M000216351

# TOGO and Leonhard

The Inspiring True Story of Alaska's Greatest
Musher and His Lead Dog

Also by

# PAM FLOWERS

*Alone across the Arctic*

*Big-Enough, Anna*

*Douggie*

*Ordinary Dogs, Extraordinary Friendships*

*Ellie's Long Walk*

*Sojo*

# TOGO and Leonhard

The inspiring true story of Alaska's greatest musher and his lead dog

*A historical novel by*

## PAM FLOWERS

Iditarod Finisher

A & A Johnston Publishing

ISBN: 978-1-57833-745-3
Library of Congress Control Number: 2020901650

Togo and Leonhard
©2020 Pamela Flowers
All rights reserved. Except for use in any review, the reproduction
or utilization of this work in whole or in part in any form by any
electronic, mechanical or other means, now known or hereafter
invented, including xerography, photocopying and recording, or in
any information storage or retrieval system, is forbidden without the
written permission of the author.

Book Design: Carmen Maldonado, Todd Communications
The typeface for this book was set in Times New Roman.

First printing March 2020

Printed in China
through **Alaska Print Brokers**, Anchorage, Alaska

Published by:     A & A Johnston Publishing
P.O. Box 188
Talkeetna, AK 99676
www.pamflowers.com

Distributed by:

Todd Communications
611 E. 12th Ave. • Anchorage, Alaska 99501-4603
(907) 274-TODD (8633) • Fax: (907) 929-5550
with other offices in Juneau and Fairbanks, Alaska
sales@toddcom.com • WWW.ALASKABOOKSANDCALENDARS.COM

*To Pam and Bob Thomas
for their dedication to the Siberian Husky*

## *Acknowledgments*

This book was made possible because of the combined efforts of many people. I would like to thank Ann Dixon, Casey Sundermann, Pam Thomas, and Kris Zuidema for reading the text and sending me helpful comments so that I could tell this story. Thank you to Sallie Greenwood for her editing. Thank you Flip Todd, Carmen Maldonado, and Mike Tucker at Todd Communications for creating the file, maps, and getting the book into print.

I would also like to thank Rachel Cohen, archivist at the Rasmuson Library at the University of Alaska Fairbanks and Amy Chan, director of the Carrie M. McLain Museum in Nome, Alaska, for helping me locate rare, invaluable, old photos and documents that I thought I might never find.

A very special thank you to Pam Thomas for her patient and thorough responses to my seemingly endless questions about Leonhard Seppala, Togo, the Siberian Husky, the Serum Relay, and many other topics too numerous to list here.

# Contents

University of Alaska Fairbanks Archive, Leonhard Seppala Collection

Togo

Sigrid Seppala Hanks Collection. Carrie M. McLain Memorial Museum
Togo and Leonhard with dog team

## CHAPTER 1

# Togo

The sled dogs sat beside their doghouses in the early morning darkness silently staring at the front door of Leonhard Seppala's cabin. The instant Leonhard opened the door and walked outside, everything changed. The dogs started running in circles and barking. Leonhard was carrying a big bucket. As he walked toward the dogs, every eye stayed locked on that bucket. They knew it was full of frozen salmon and big chunks of tallow. When Leonhard was about three feet from the first dog, he grabbed a salmon and tossed it into the air. Before it landed on the snow, the hungry dog snatched the salmon out of midair with its mouth, chomped a few times, and wolfed it down. Leonhard dropped a chunk of tallow beside the dog and then moved on to the next dog, and the next, and the next. By the time the last dog was fed, the first dog had already finished eating and was digging around in search of any tiny morsel that might be hidden in the snow.

A couple of minutes later Constance, Leonhard's wife, heard the familiar sound of something being dragged across the front porch. The door flew open. Leonhard hauled his dog sled through the doorway and plunked it down. The sled was covered with a frosty layer of snow and almost filled the tiny, brightly lit parlor. Without bothering to close the door, he went back outside and brought in all the lines and dog harnesses. Leonhard carefully spread the lines over the sled and draped the harnesses over the furniture before finally closing the door. Constance was used to Leonhard doing this and went on cooking breakfast.

Heat from the cook stove quickly warmed the room back up as Leonhard and Constance sat down to eat breakfast. "How far will you run the dogs today?" asked Constance.

"Oh, around 30 miles. They've been working pretty hard pulling freight and passengers around all winter. I don't see why we need any more long runs. The race is just ten days away, so I figure eight days of short runs and then we'll stay home and rest."

As usual, Leonhard bolted down his breakfast and then got up and walked over to the sled which was now sitting in a puddle of water. He looked back at Constance and said with a little smile, "I'm gonna win The Sweeps, you know."

Constance smiled gently and nodded, "I know."

Leonhard carefully inspected every line and harness looking for anything that was frayed or worn out. Then he ran his hands over every inch of the sled. The runners, handlebar, and basket were all in perfect condition. Over in the kitchen Constance lifted a huge pot of cooked beans off the stove and put it on the table. While the beans cooled, she started frying hamburgers. Hamburger and beans were Leonhard's favorite trail foods. By noon she had carefully packaged everything into meal-sized portions and put them outside to freeze.

It was March and all this was in preparation for Leonhard to compete in the 1916 All Alaska Sweepstakes Race, commonly called The Sweeps. At 408 miles, it was the longest and most challenging sled dog race in Alaska. When Leonhard was satisfied that everything was in good shape, he hauled the sled back outside. The moment the dogs saw the sled they went wild again, barking and howling, and running around in circles.

University of Alaska Fairbanks Archive, Leonhard Seppala Collection
Leonhard Seppala racing in Fairbanks, Alaska

Leonhard neatly laid out 16 harnesses on the snow in a long line in front of the sled. Every dog strained toward Leonhard as if they were saying, *Pick me! Pick me!* Lead dog Russky was the first to get harnessed. One by one, Leonhard brought the dogs over until all 16 dogs were ready to go. The dogs lunged and pulled at their lines. Leonhard climbed onto the back of the sled, lifted the snowhook, and called, "All right!" In that instant every dog fell silent. The team tore off down the trail. The dogs left behind stood like a bunch of little statues as they watched their buddies disappear in the distance.

With all that was happening, no one noticed that one of the dogs near the back of the kennel was giving birth. Inside her doghouse, Dolly, the puppy's mother, curled herself around her newborn puppy to keep him warm. She gently coaxed him to nurse. Every time he tried to swallow, he cried.

Constance had known that Dolly was due to deliver soon and just yesterday she had put a big pile of fresh straw inside Dolly's doghouse to help keep her warm. As soon as Leonhard left, she hurried over to the kennel to check on her. When she kneeled beside Dolly's doghouse and looked inside, she saw only one, very, tiny puppy. Dolly looked up at Constance with a furrowed brow. Something was wrong.

Constance knew a lot about puppies and dogs. When she saw that the puppy was having trouble swallowing, she knew this was serious. Newborn puppies need to eat every two or three hours, otherwise they will quickly die. Constance gently picked him up and checked him over. She discovered a swelling in his throat. She got a warm compress and held it against his neck for a few minutes. After that he could swallow a little but he still needed help. For the next several days, every few hours day and night,

Constance made time in her hectic life to hold the puppy in her arms and apply warm compresses to his neck. After a few days the swelling disappeared and he was able to swallow without pain.

Between Dolly and Constance doting on him, the little puppy quickly got used to being the center of attention. At about four weeks of age, he stuck his head out the door of his mother's doghouse. It was one small step for a puppy but one long tumble headfirst into the soft snow. Not the least bit frightened, he managed to explore all of two feet before Dolly reached down, plucked him up by the scruff of his neck, and hauled him back inside their house. By eight weeks, he was tearing around the kennel playing with the big dogs and nipping at their toes. By the time he was four months old, the puppy was already roaming the tundra by himself. With no supervision or guidance on how to behave, he got used to doing pretty much as he pleased.

Leonhard was too busy getting ready for the race to pay much attention to the puppy. But he noticed how confident and feisty he was for one so young. After a little thought, he decided to name him Togo, after a famous admiral in the Japanese navy.

CHAPTER 2

# Togo Finds a New Home

In sled dog kennels young dogs not ready to begin training are often allowed to run loose behind teams when they take off down the trail. They usually can't keep up for long. As they get left farther and farther behind, the pups give up and walk back to the kennel. Not Togo. Not only did he not go back, Togo figured out that if he left *before* a team set out he could hunker down somewhere along the trail and lay in wait. As the team passed by, Togo would leap up and bite the lead dog's ear. Then he would run away before his victim could bite him back.

One evening as Constance and Leonhard were eating dinner, Leonhard complained, "It makes me so mad when Togo does this. I know it's painful for the dog he bites. Today the dogs got so upset they left the trail and took off after him right across the tundra. It took me forever to get them under control. We were supposed to be working but instead we ended up chasing that dog."

"How often does he do this?" asked Constance.

"Every day!" answered Leonhard.

"You're going to have to figure something out, Leonhard."

A couple of days later a friend stopped by for a visit and mentioned that she was looking for a pet dog. Leonhard looked at Constance and a big smile spread across his face.

"My friend, we have the perfect dog for you. Let's go outside and you can have a look at him."

Togo was a curious looking dog. He had a thick coat that was a mixture of tan, brown, and black, with a few white hairs scattered here and there giving him an odd sort of gray color. On his chest was a big patch of whitish fur and the lower part of his legs were white. As husky puppies grow up, both their ears usually stand straight up. Togo's left ear stood up but his right ear stayed slightly tipped, giving him a sort of cute, puppy look.

Out in the dog lot, Leonhard, Constance, and the woman gathered around Togo. He loved being the center of attention. When the woman smiled at him, he pulled his lips back in a big, doggy smile.

"Ah, what a sweet face," said the woman. "I think he'll make a perfect pet."

At his new home Togo was given a comfortable doghouse and fed lots of steaks. The woman decided it was too cold for him to live outside, so she brought him

Sigrid Seppala Hanks Collection, Carrie M. McLain Memorial Museum
A young Togo (ca. 1917)

into her house so he could enjoy the warmth of the parlor. The woman didn't know much about dogs. But she was convinced that, given a little time, Togo would learn to appreciate her kindness and become a model pet. Of course, none of this mattered one whit to Togo. He certainly enjoyed wolfing down all those steaks but had no interest whatsoever in becoming a pet. Anytime she drew near, he would back away and snarl. Whenever she tried to pet him, Togo would bare his teeth and snap at her. He kept walking over to the front door where he would bark, demanding to be let out. When the woman refused to open the door, Togo would growl. It was not a happy situation.

One day the woman went off to the store and left Togo alone inside. Used to making decisions on his own, Togo decided this was his chance to escape. He raced across the parlor, hurled himself through the front window, and ran back to Leonhard's kennel! Leonhard promptly returned Togo to the woman. He told her, "Chain him up to his doghouse outside until he understands that this is his new home."

Togo would not have it!

Somehow that very night Togo got loose and once again ran back to the kennel. When Leonhard opened the door the next morning and saw Togo sitting on the front porch, he called Constance over. "It looks like our little escapee has done it again."

Constance looked down at Togo who was sitting there wagging his tail and said, "I guess he's made up his mind that this is his home."

Leonhard couldn't help but smile. "Well, he's got a few faults but I sort of missed the little rascal."

"So did I," replied Constance. "Togo, it looks like you're here to stay."

Togo pulled his lips back in a big smile as though he understood what had just been decided.

## CHAPTER 3

# Togo Learns a Hard Lesson

Although Togo was born in Leonhard Seppala's kennel, he was owned by a man named Victor Anderson who was Leonhard's boss at work. Anderson and Leonhard worked for a gold mining company called Pioneer Mining Company. If the men weren't busy delivering supplies by dog team to gold mines, they were running sled dog races.

When Togo was about six months old, Anderson decided to see if he was ready to begin training to become a sled dog. He found Togo so unruly and difficult to work with that he gave him to the Seppalas. They liked the little fellow, but Togo was small even by Siberian Husky standards and he didn't look as though he would be strong enough to work in a freight-hauling team. Not only that, Togo was short in the body and Leonhard figured he wouldn't be fast enough for a racing team. No one expected anything from Togo.

Togo was still running around biting dogs on their ears. Before Leonhard could figure out what to do about him, something happened that would cure Togo of this bad behavior for the rest of his life. On that fateful day as Togo lay in wait for Leonhard's team to pass by, Togo spotted a team of Malamutes coming down the trail from the opposite direction. He shifted his attention to the Malamutes. Togo could see that the Malamutes were bigger than Leonhard's dogs but what Togo didn't know was that Malamutes could be a lot meaner. He hunkered down and waited for the right moment to launch his attack. Just as the lead Malamute passed by, Togo leaped up, grabbed the dog's ear, and bit down hard.

In a flash the dog snatched Togo by the scruff of his neck and tossed him into the air like a rag doll. Togo landed with a thud. He was shocked and dazed. Before he could run away, the angry dog sank her teeth into his neck and shook him violently back and forth.

Leonhard could see what was happening and urged his team to speed up. The instant he arrived, Leonhard leaped off his sled and ran toward the Malamutes shouting, "No! No!" Leonhard grabbed Togo by the back legs and tried to pull him away, but the dog jerked Togo right out of Leonhard's hands. The other Malamutes closed in on Togo and went into a frenzy, mobbing him, and tearing at him with their teeth. Togo screamed in pain.

Leonhard could do nothing but watch in horror.

The Malamute dog driver jumped off his sled and waded into the mayhem, yelling "No! Get off. Get off!"

One by one, the powerful man pulled his dogs off Togo, throwing them left and right. But no sooner did he pull one dog off than another dog charged right back into the brawl. The Malamutes were so crazed, some of them started attacking each other. Finally, the fighting took its toll. Chests heaving and exhausted, the Malamutes started backing off one by one. The Malamutes' driver was very angry. He cursed as he shoved his dogs around and straightened the team out. Without saying a word to Leonhard, the man stepped onto his sled and drove away.

Togo's bloodied body lay motionless on the snow, his eyes closed. Leonhard stepped forward and whispered softly, "Togo? … Togo?" There was no response. Leonhard gently placed his hand on Togo's chest. He felt his chest rising and falling. Togo was breathing. Togo was alive! Togo tried to open his eyes, but his little face was too badly swollen. Togo was so chewed up all he could do was lie there. Leonhard gently lifted him into his arms and whispered, "I'm sorry, Togo." He whimpered as Leonhard carefully placed him in the sled. Togo hated riding in the sled basket but this time he didn't complain.

Back home, Constance cleaned Togo up, bandaged his wounds, and once again patiently nursed him back to health.

It was a hard lesson for Togo but what he learned on that terrible day would serve him well in the future. Teaching a lead dog how to pass another team without becoming entangled or getting into a fight is always a challenge. But later, when he joined Leonhard's team, Togo already knew that when he saw a team coming, he should always do his best to stay clear.

CHAPTER 4

# Togo Escapes

In November, one of Leonhard's bosses, Louis Stevenson, wanted to go to Dime Creek to look at a gold strike. Leonhard gave strict instructions to his kennel manager, "Mr. Stevenson wants to get up to Dime Creek really fast. We don't have time to mess around with Togo chasing after us and causing trouble. You keep that dog in the kennel until we get back!"

Togo stood quietly watching Leonhard as he harnessed the team and took off down the trail. He didn't look disappointed but that was because he had no intentions of being left behind. A few hours later, just after dark, Togo decided it was time to make his escape and go find Leonhard. Never mind that the entire kennel was surrounded by a seven-foot high fence. Togo had made up his mind that he was leaving and that's all there was to that. He stood in the middle of the kennel, ran full speed toward the fence, and launched himself skyward. Just as he was about to clear the top, Togo's back left leg got caught in the fence.

Togo was now dangling seven feet in the air, on the outside of the kennel, upside down! He kicked and squirmed and twisted every which way but he could not get loose. The fence wire started cutting into Togo's leg. Yikes, that hurt! Togo squealed in a high pitched voice. "Yip! Yip!" The more he struggled the deeper the wire cut his leg. "Yip! Yip!"

Of course Togo's cries set off every dog in the kennel and soon everyone was barking. The kennel manager woke up and ran outside. "What's going on out here?" the man shouted. He searched all over with his flashlight and finally spotted Togo. "What the? How did you get up there?" The man ran back inside his cabin and grabbed a pair of wire cutters. "Hold still," he shouted at the squirming dog. "Hold still, I said." It was a long reach but the man managed to snip the wire that was holding Togo's leg. Togo dropped to the ground with a thud. No matter that his leg was gushing blood, Togo leaped to his feet, and raced off into the night.

"Come back here!" shouted the man.

Togo paid no attention. Togo was on a mission. Togo was going to find Leonhard Seppala!

By that evening Leonhard and his boss had reached

the roadhouse in Solomon, about 32 miles from Leonhard's home. While they slept in cozy, warm beds, a storm moved in. Late that night Togo made it to the roadhouse. He hunkered down in the snow and tried to stay warm. The next morning Leonhard and his boss set out before daylight. Leonhard noticed that the dogs took off faster than usual and seemed to be excited by something up ahead on the trail. The wind was blowing hard and kicking up so much snow that Leonhard could hardly see beyond his lead dog. After a few minutes, he shouted to Mr. Stevenson over the roar of the wind, "The dogs must smell reindeer, otherwise they would have settled into a slower pace by now."

As the sun rose over a cloudy sky, the wind slowly died down and Leonhard spotted the cause of the dog's excitement. "Look, there's a fox up ahead. That's what they've been chasing." But as they drew a little closer Leonhard was puzzled. Something wasn't right. "What is that?" he asked in a low voice. He stuck his head forward and squinted, trying to see through the gray light. Leonhard could hardly believe his eyes. "What on earth?" he exclaimed! "That's no fox, that's Togo!"

In that moment, Togo leaped onto the trail and ran towards lead dog, Russky. "Togo, no! Don't you bite Russky's ear!" Quick as a wink, Togo nipped the leader on his ear, spun around, and raced back down the trail. The entire team leaped into action and charged after the little dog. As fast as they ran, Togo was faster and they couldn't catch him. After a couple of miles, Leonhard managed to slow the team down and stopped. Mr. Stevenson shouted, "Leonhard, what is this? Why are we racing down the trail chasing some loose dog?"

Leonhard was a little embarrassed. "Well," he said, "you did say you wanted to get there fast."

Togo stopped a ways down the trail. He put his front legs down flat on the snow with his back legs still standing up in a play bow. His big bushy tail waved back and forth through the air. He pulled his lips back in a huge smile. Togo was so happy to be with Leonhard again, he playfully barked, "Woof!"

Leonard, however, was not so happy. He glared at the dog and demanded, "Togo! How did you get out of the kennel?"

"Woof!"

Only then did Leonhard notice there was blood on Togo's leg. Leonhard's voice could be gentle and forceful all at the same time. "What's the matter with your leg, Togo? Come over here and let me look at it." Leonhard didn't have many first aid supplies to work with, but he fixed Togo's leg as best he could. "Well, we've come too far to take you back to the kennel. I guess you'll just have to come along with us." Togo's leg was a little stiff and swollen but he was still able to run loose beside the team.

## CHAPTER 5

# Togo Makes the Team

The next day Togo was in fine fiddle, so it didn't take long for him to get in trouble. No sooner had they started down the trail when Togo spotted some reindeer grazing quietly out on the tundra. He stopped and stood perfectly still, staring at the herd.

Leonhard Seppala knew dogs and he knew exactly what Togo was thinking. Leonhard turned his head slightly to the right and looked at Togo out of the corners of his eyes. Togo turned his head and looked at Leonhard out of the corners of his eyes. For a moment they both stood staring at one another. Leonhard clenched his teeth and said in a gruff voice, "Togo, no! DO NOT chase those reindeer!"

It was no use. In a flash, Togo tore off after the reindeer. The other dogs decided this was way too much fun to miss out on. The entire team swung off the trail and joined the chase. In an instant the team was completely out of control. The only thing Leonhard could do was hang on to the handlebar and hope his boss didn't get bucked out of the sled. But the reindeer were swift runners and after a couple of miles they disappeared in the distance leaving the dogs far behind.

Finally, Leonhard was able to regain control over the team. He was furious. Leonhard decided that once and for all something had to be done about Togo. He drove the team back onto the trail and stopped. Togo was standing about 50 feet away with that big smile on his face. In a no-nonsense voice Leonhard ordered, "Togo, come here!" The smile slipped off Togo's face. He knew he was in big trouble. He jerked his head left then right and his eyes flitted all over the place, trying to look as though he hadn't heard Leonhard.

Leonhard was in no mood to put up with any more foolishness. Leonhard's eyes flashed as he glared at Togo. "Togo, I know you can hear me. I said come here!" Togo took a deep breath. He kept his eyes and head down as he slowly slunk over and sat down at Leonhard's feet. Without saying a word, Leonhard took Togo by the collar, led him over to the sled, reached into his sled bag, pulled out a harness, put it on the little dog, and hooked him to the gangline right in front of the sled. And just like that, Togo was a sled dog.

Leonhard walked back and climbed onto the sled. "All right, let's go!"

He was surprised to see Togo lean into his harness and pull. "Would you look at that?"

Leonhard said to Mr. Stevenson. "Togo has never been in a team before today. He's not the least bit confused. In fact, he's working like a veteran sled dog."

"Let's see how he does after a few miles," cautioned Mr. Stevenson.

Leonhard kept a close eye on Togo. He figured that because Togo was pulling so hard, he would soon tire and have to be carried in the sled. But incredibly, Togo kept up the pace and was soon working harder than any of the other dogs. After a few miles Leonhard promoted Togo by moving him farther up in the team. Lead dog, Russky, was well-behaved and one of Leonhard's best leaders. He thought Russky would be a fine example for Togo and would help him learn how to behave. So several miles before they reached Dime Creek, Leonhard stopped the team and moved Togo up beside Russky. Togo took to the lead position as though he had been running there his entire life.

For some time Leonhard had been pondering the fact that most of his lead dogs were getting older and he would soon need younger dogs to take their place. He watched Togo running effortlessly mile after mile. By the time they reached Dime Creek, Togo had traveled 75 miles on his first day in harness! Mr. Stevenson got out of the sled and nodded toward Togo.

"That little dog did okay."

Leonhard had a huge smile on his face and said, "He sure did. Pretty amazing for an eight-month old puppy." This little 48-pound runt, that had been nothing more than a nuisance, had shown intelligence, speed, strength, and endurance. Leonhard knew he had found something in Togo that he needed — a natural born leader.

On that cold, November day, Togo got something he needed — a place in a dog team and someone who was willing to give him a chance to show what he could do.

That evening, as Leonhard watched Togo wolf down salmon and tallow, he made himself a promise. He would drive Togo carefully and sparingly and never ask for more than he could give. This would be the best decision that Leonhard Seppala ever made as a dog musher, for the time would come when Togo would play a part in something more important than anyone could ever imagine.

CHAPTER 6

# Leonhard Seppala's Early Life

Leonhard Seppala hadn't always been such a good judge of sled dogs. In fact, his life didn't even begin in Alaska. He was born on September 14, 1877, in a village on Skjervøy island about 240 miles north of the Arctic Circle in Norway. His mother, Ane, was a very active and surprisingly strong woman with a talent for weaving. She ran a neat and disciplined home. His father, Isak, was a blacksmith, coppersmith, brass molder, and all-around mechanic during the summer, and a cod fisherman in the North Sea during the winter months. The family grew in size and by the time Leonhard was 11 years old he had two younger brothers and two younger sisters.

As the oldest son, Leonhard began learning his father's trade. During his first year at the blacksmith shop Leonhard made himself a harpoon. His father didn't make him work all day and encouraged Leonhard's strong sense of adventure. Almost every day he would take his harpoon, hop in his small boat, and row out into the middle of the harbor. He would sit and wait patiently for dolphins to show up. Dolphins are a kind of whale and Leonhard imagined himself a great whaling captain. When dolphins swam past, Leonhard threw the harpoon again and again. Happily for the dolphins, Leonhard's imagination was greater than his skill with a harpoon. Never once did he manage to spear a dolphin in all his days in the harbor.

Like most Norwegians, Leonhard was an avid skier and loved to spend time with his friends skiing on the snowy slopes around Skjervøy. His favorite sport was wrestling. Though Leonhard was small for his age, he was quick and agile, and usually won most matches.

At age 12 his father took him fishing in the North Sea for the first time. The work was exhausting, brutally cold, and dangerous. Leonhard's mother hated to see her son and husband leave. For the next two winters, Ane convinced her husband to let Leonhard stay home so he could continue his education. But when Leonhard turned 15 his father insisted that he go fishing again. All winter there was storm after storm. During most of those storms at least one boat would sink into the icy waters, its fishermen never to be seen again. When he returned home that year, Leonhard vowed this would not be his life.

Just before he turned 16, Leonhard moved to Norway's capital of Kristiania, which reverted to the name

Oslo in 1925. Despite his skill as a blacksmith, Leonhard could not find work. He needed to earn money to support himself. Finally, he took the only job he could get, cleaning and repairing boilers, a kind of tank for heating water.

It wasn't just the chance to be out on his own that attracted Leonhard to Kristiania. One of his friends, Margit, also from Skjervøy, had moved there several months earlier. It didn't take long for Leonhard to find her and soon they were spending all their free time together. After a few weeks they began making plans and talking about marriage. But life was a tough struggle in Kristiania and Leonhard thought he should move back to Skjervøy and try to get himself better established. Less than a year later, Margit developed pneumonia and died.

Life continued uneventfully for Leonhard until one day a friend of his, Jafet Lindeberg, showed up in town. Jafet was well educated, spoke five languages, and was an impressive, hard-working, highly-motivated young man. Some years back he had traveled to Alaska and gone prospecting for gold with two other men. Together they struck it rich and formed the Pioneer Mining Company. Jafet was a very wealthy man when he returned to visit Skjervøy. Leonhard and three friends gathered around a table and listened for hours to Jafet's stories of riches in Alaska. It didn't take long for the four young men to develop a strong case of gold fever. With nothing to tie them down, they decide to go to Alaska and seek their fortune. The only problem was they didn't have any money to get there.

Jafet looked at his friends. He could see their dreams written all over their faces. Jafet was a kind and generous man and made them an offer. "Tell you what, I'll loan each of you enough money to pay your passage to Alaska. When you get there, I'll give all of you jobs so you can pay me back."

"Wow! This is the chance of a lifetime!" said Leonhard. "What do you say, fellas?" Everyone was thrilled to accept Jafet's offer. Handshakes all around sealed the deal and the four young men began planning their journey to the land of big dreams and promised wealth.

## CHAPTER 7

# Alaskan Dreams

Leonhard and his three friends got tickets on a passenger ship and sailed across the Atlantic to New York City. From there they boarded a train and traveled across the United States to Seattle, Washington. Another ship carried them north. On June 24, 1900, Leonhard Seppala and his three friends arrived in Nome, Alaska.

The town was bustling and packed with people who had come north to seek their fortunes in the gold fields. At first Leonhard and his friends tried their hand at prospecting but they had no luck. Leonhard was mindful of his debt and went to see Jafet. True to his word, Jafet gave Leonhard a job. The job was working nights shoveling gravel near a big ditch where gold was filtered through a screening system. Even though Leonhard had strong arms from working as a blacksmith, he still found the work exhausting. The shifts were ten hours long. By the end of his first shift Leonhard's hands and arms hurt so much he

University of Alaska Fairbanks Archive, Leonhard Seppala Collection

Ships were required to anchor offshore about one and one half to two miles because there was no harbor in Nome. Passengers climbed onto a platform that was raised off the beach with a crane and then swung over and lowered onto a barge known as a lighter. Once all the passengers were on the lighter, they were moved out to the ship.

couldn't sleep that night. He knew that some men didn't last even one shift. He also knew that if he quit there were plenty of men looking for work who would gladly take his place. Leonhard was determined not to give up no matter how much he hurt. Besides, he didn't know how else to make money.

During the summer months the tundra around Nome thawed and was soft, wet, and spongy and almost impossible to travel across. But as long as it stayed that way, gold mining continued and Leonhard kept shoveling. As fall pushed summer away, the temperatures dropped until the land froze and mining stopped for the winter. Once again Jafet remembered his friend and appointed Leonhard night watchman. Theft was very common in the gold fields. His new job was to keep an eye on the mining equipment and make certain it wasn't stolen during the idle winter months. This was perfect because it allowed him to not only earn an income, but he could spend his days skiing.

Not everything related to mining stopped during the winter. Jafet had heard about a possible gold strike several miles from Nome. On a cold day in December 1900 Jafet sent Leonhard and three other employees, Andrew, Fred, and John, out to see if the strike was real. Jafet purchased 13 dogs for them to use. There were 11 Malamutes and two mongrel dogs. The mongrel dogs were brothers and they were huge. One dog weighed 120 pounds and the other 110. Leonhard Seppala was a laborer, not a dog musher, but he was willing to try.

As the four men and dogs set out, the weather was fairly calm. Though the temperature was below zero, it wasn't too cold to travel. On December 24 they came across a big flock of ptarmigan and managed to hunt enough birds for every man and dog to enjoy a huge feast.

They even managed to rustle up some rice pudding and had themselves a tasty Christmas Eve dinner. They soon reached the site where the gold strike was supposed to be. Leonhard said, "Andrew, how about you and I set up camp here and see if we can find any gold?" "Fine with me," said Andrew. Fred and John talked between themselves. Then Fred said, "Okay, John and I are going on a few miles farther, so we'll take the dogs with us." The men wished each other good luck as Fred and John took off.

Every day was a struggle. The temperature dropped to -40°F and they were plagued by endless blizzards. To dig into the frozen ground they had to gather willow branches and build a fire to thaw the earth. They would then dig until they hit frozen ground and then repeat the process over and over. By mid-January, when Fred and John had found no gold, they decided to call it quits and went back to Nome. They took the eleven Malamutes with them but left the two big dogs with Andrew and Leonhard. When Leonhard checked the dogs over, he was appalled at how thin they were and set about feeding and caring for them. After several days the dogs were healthy again and strong enough to work. Leonhard hooked them up to a small hand-sled and drove them around to pick up loads of willow branches for firewood. He was amazed at how hard they worked and appreciated that they made the chore much faster and easier.

On the first of February the temperature dropped to -60°F. Their supplies were dwindling and they had found no gold. So Andrew and Leonhard decided it was time to return to Nome. Not wanting to over-burden the dogs, they loaded their hand-sled with a large sleeping bag, one shovel, and the small amount of food they had left. They hitched up the two dogs and took off.

At first they traveled over hard-packed snow and made good time, but it didn't take long for them to get into trouble. After a few miles they ran into soft, deep snow. Walking was exhausting for the men, but the big, furry brothers just kept plugging along. When they broke through ice into freezing water that soaked the men to their knees, the brothers carried on as though nothing had happened. Just when they thought it couldn't get any worse, another blizzard came up. The men started to freeze. If they were to survive, they needed to find shelter fast. After a few steps the men stumbled over a huge snowdrift that blocked the wind. They dropped to their knees and began digging, Andrew with the shovel and Leonhard with his hands. Within minutes they had a small cave dug in the side of the snowdrift. The two men and dogs crawled inside. It was freezing cold in the cave but Andrew and Leonhard were grateful to be out of the wind.

The dogs were not so grateful. The cave was too warm for them because of their heavy coats. They decided to crawl back outside. The dogs wanted to stay close to Leonhard so they plopped down on top of the cave. The roof instantly collapsed, burying Andrew and Leonhard!

Between the weight of the dogs and snow packed around them, the men were smothering. Nearly panicked, they frantically clawed their way out of the cave. Back in the full force of the blizzard, they knew they needed to start moving or they would freeze to death. As they struggled through the blowing snow, they had no way of knowing which direction they were heading. Within minutes they were lost. Leonhard was so cold he couldn't feel his hands or feet. He figured they were done for. All of a sudden the dogs took off running. "Come back here!" shouted Leonhard. The dogs paid no attention. Andrew and Leonhard chased after the dogs. Their sleeping bag and food were on that sled. They had to catch the dogs or they would surely die! Just when it seemed they would never catch up, a huge shadow loomed up in front of them. A few more steps and they realized they were standing in front of the Sliskovitch Roadhouse.

Andrew and Leonhard stumbled through the doorway. The owner told them to sit down by the stove and gave each of them a cup of hot coffee. The roadhouse was nothing more than a canvas tent about the size of a small bedroom that was nearly buried under a snowdrift.

The men didn't care how primitive the place was. It was warm and they were grateful to be alive. They realized the dogs had apparently smelled food and decided to rescue themselves. The brothers were quite happy to sleep out in the storm and wait as long as they knew Leonhard was inside.

The next day Andrew and Leonhard woke up to find the blizzard gone and the temperature had risen to -40°F. They hooked up the dogs and happily set out for Nome. The rest of their journey was uneventful. Leonhard was impressed by how hard the two dogs had worked and how they always took their hardships in stride. When he told Jafet Lindeberg that the dogs had saved their lives, Jafet gave them to Leonhard. The brothers never ran off again.

It was because of those two dogs that Leonhard Seppala fell in love with dogs and dog mushing. He would later say, "To them I owe my great compassion for dogs, worth more to me than all the trophies I won as a champion dog musher. To those mongrels I owe my first great lesson in mutual trust and respect which is the only worthwhile relationship between man and his four-legged friends. From them I learned the value of patience and the real worth of companionship."

CHAPTER 8

# Leonhard Becomes a Dog Musher

Over the next few years a lot of things happened in Leonhard's life. He worked his way up through various jobs at the Pioneer Mining Company and became a supervisor. He learned to run big dog teams and started hauling passengers and supplies around the Seward Peninsula and out to the mines. He loved dogs and quickly discovered that he had a knack for working with them. He enjoyed getting to know each dog, learning its strengths and weaknesses, and where it fit best in the team. A big part of his job was to make sure they had enough good food, plenty of water even on the coldest winter days, and that their kennel was kept clean. Leonhard took pride in keeping the dogs happy and healthy. The work was hard, cold, and often meant spending long days on the trail. But as usual, no matter what happened, he never complained and never quit. Leonhard Seppala just got the job done.

Leonhard seemed to have a never ending need to excel. He had those three things everyone needs to be a success. He found something he was good at, he worked very hard, and he was willing to take risks. With his drive, it didn't take long before Leonhard Seppala was considered the best dog driver at the Pioneer Mining Company.

In 1906 Leonhard became a citizen of the United States. Another change soon entered Leonhard's personal life. There were far more men than women working around the gold mining camps. One day while Leonhard was working at a camp, he noticed a young woman who was working as a waitress. He found out that her name was Constance and that she had recently emigrated from Belgium. He saw several young men spending most of their off-time in the kitchen helping her wash dishes. Not to be outdone, Leonhard started visiting Constance every time he got the chance. Over the next year, they grew to like each other and one day Leonhard said, "I've been thinking you and I should get married."

Constance replied, "Well, that's rather interesting as I have been thinking along the same lines."

Within minutes Leonhard had his dog team harnessed and drove Constance into town where they got married.

Because people kept arriving in Nome to seek their fortunes, more and more dog teams were put into use. The inevitable happened. People began bragging about whose team was the fastest. Soon they were having little races all over the place. Of course people then started betting on who would win these races. A man named Albert Fink noticed that some people weren't treating their dogs very well. He wanted that stopped and came up with a clever idea. In 1908 he got together with some people in Nome and formed the Nome Kennel Club. The club members set up the All Alaska Sweepstakes Race. The first place prize was $10,000! To show racers they meant business about the proper care of sled dogs, they wrote a list of rules. The toughest and most important rule stated "The cruel and inhumane treatment by any driver is strictly prohibited, under penalty of losing the race and forfeiture of the owner's team."

The course would go from Nome to Candle and back to Nome, covering a distance of 408 miles. The route would follow the telegraph lines through a series of villages. This meant team positions could be reported frequently. That made people who were betting on the teams happy. More importantly, it would allow officials to closely monitor how the racers were treating their dogs.

Ten teams signed up. Their progress over the race trail was posted on a huge chalkboard in the Board of Trade Saloon, located on Front Street in downtown Nome. Bets were constantly being made on who would be the winner. The All Alaska Sweepstakes Race was a huge success. It quickly developed into a winter carnival and the racers became big celebrities. Leonhard didn't consider himself a racer but he admired the men who dared to compete and envied their courage. Every evening after work he would hurry down to the saloon to see who was in what position. Even after the race was over, Leonhard would hang around hoping to just stand next to one of the racers. If he was lucky, maybe he would even get a chance to talk with one or two.

As the sport of dog racing grew in popularity, so did interest in the Siberian Husky. In March 1913 a fur trader from Nome named Max Gottschalk sailed his ship across the Bering Sea to Siberia, where he purchased 16 Siberian Huskies. Somehow, before he was able to sail home, his ship sank. If he was going to get back home alive, he was going to have to save himself. So, Max Gottschalk did the only thing he could think of. He would travel home by dog team. He hooked the dogs up to a sled and headed north along the coast. When he reached a place where the sea was frozen, he headed east across the ice toward Alaska. Until then, no one had ever crossed the Bering Sea by dog team. Little things like the fact that he didn't know how far the ice stretched, or that the ice could break up at any time, or that he might have a run-in with a polar bear didn't matter to Max Gottschalk. He just wanted to get home. Luck was with him as he drove the dog team from Cape Dezhnev, Siberia across the frozen Bering Sea

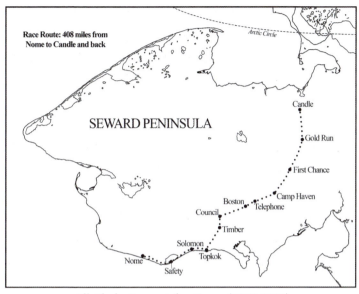

All Alaska Sweepstakes Races (1908-1917)

to Shishmaref, Alaska. It was a distance of about 103 miles and took him nine days. From there he sledded along the coast of the Seward Peninsula to Nome. Max Gottschalk made history by completing the first and only known crossing of the Bering Sea by dog team.

    As it happened, there was a dog on that team named Dolly. Sometime during the winter of 1913—1914 she was sold to Victor Anderson. In her first known litter she gave birth to six puppies. In her second litter, most likely in 1916, Dolly gave birth to one puppy. That puppy was Togo.

    Besides dog racing, this was also the era of polar

exploration. The life of one of the explorers would have considerable impact on Leonhard Seppala. In 1911—1912 Roald Amundsen and three other men mushed dogs across part of Antarctica to the South Pole. Now Amundsen planned to dog mush to the North Pole in 1914. He was close friends with Jafet Lindeberg and asked Jafet to acquire dogs for the expedition. In 1913 Jafet, Victor Anderson, and Leonhard spent a great deal of time searching the Nome area, finding and buying several young Siberian Huskies. Jafet placed all the dogs in Leonhard's kennel and told him to start training them for the North Pole expedition. Being Norwegian himself, Leonhard felt honored and was thrilled to have the opportunity to train dogs for Roald Amundsen.

A few months later Amundsen wrote to Jafet and explained that he had not been able to raise enough money to go to the North Pole and had to cancel the expedition. The dogs were left in Leonhard's kennel and he continued training them. He discovered that the Siberian Huskies were slow starters but would quickly settle into a good pace that they could maintain for miles and miles without growing tired. They had excellent coats, good feet, and unlike Malamutes, were not prone to fighting. He would later say, "I literally fell in love with them from the start."

## CHAPTER 9

# Leonhard's First Sled Dog Race

During the winter of 1913—1914, several people around Nome had been paying attention as Leonhard trained the Siberians. Some people were impressed with the dogs and a few even suggested to Leonhard that he enter The Sweeps. Leonhard was flattered. However, up until 1914 he had only used dogs for freighting and transporting passengers. It had never occurred to him to enter the race. He knew his freight dogs were not fast enough to compete. The only dogs he thought might possibly be considered race dogs were the young and inexperienced Siberian Huskies. But he seriously doubted they were ready for the 408 mile race. A couple of mushers suggested that Leonhard enter the Loyal Order of the Moose Burden Race. It went from Nome to Safety and back, a total distance of only 84 miles. Each musher was required to carry a passenger or 100 pounds in their sled. This would be a good test for the Siberians.

So it came to be that on February 9, 1914, Leonhard Seppala found himself at the starting line of his first ever sled dog race. The dogs started out running well but certainly not at a winning pace. After about four miles, Leonhard glanced over his shoulder and saw the racer behind him was running beside his sled. And he was catching up! While he was still looking back, Leonhard's dogs suddenly gave a jerk and nearly pulled the handlebar out of his hands

Enter the bird.

Leonhard looked around to see what had excited the dogs. There, about a hundred yards ahead, just sitting on the trail, was a raven. The chase was on!

The dogs sped up so fast, all Leonhard could do was hang on. Just as the dogs were closing in on the raven, the bird decided it was time to take wing. Only it didn't fly away, it glided ever so slowly right in front of the team just a few feet above the trail. Ravens are smart birds and teasing dog teams is fun for them. Again and again it took wing, flying, landing, flying, landing. All the while the dogs kept running as fast as their legs could carry them. The bird always managed to stay just out of reach. The raven landed again on the trail, but this time it just sat there watching the team race towards it.

"Caw, caw!" called the raven, as if to say, *Come on, just try to catch me!* The dogs were crazed with excitement.

This time they were going to catch that bird. "Caw, caw," the raven teased. The dogs had been chasing the raven for nearly four miles. Now they were just a few feet away! Still the raven sat on the trail. In a final burst of speed, the lead dogs pounced. In the last possible moment, the raven launched itself skyward, escaping the canine jaws of death. With one last teasing "Caw, caw" it flew away over the distant hills. Never mind that the bird was now nothing more than a feathered fantasy. The dogs were so excited, that they kept right on speeding down the trail.

Eventually the dogs did slow down and Leonhard took the mandatory four-hour layover at Safety before heading back to Nome. Leonhard's team had run faster than any other team. Leonhard Seppala had won his first sled dog race. He would later say, "I have always attributed my start in dog racing to the raven on the trail, for the winning of that race inspired me to begin my career as a dog racer."

A lot of people in Nome believed that Leonhard's victory was a fluke. But members of the Nome Kennel Club were impressed and they urged Leonhard to enter the 1914 All Alaska Sweepstakes Race. Even the famous sled dog musher, Scotty Allen, told Leonhard his team was good enough for the race. Leonhard still thought his dogs were too young. "Besides", he complained, "what with all the extra dog food and equipment, it costs a lot of money just to train. I'm very busy at work this time of year and I don't have time to prepare."

But people kept encouraging him and the idea kept rattling around in his brain. One day Leonhard asked a trusted friend, "What do you think? Should I enter The Sweeps?"

"You may not win this time. But some day you may," his friend said.

This got Leonhard thinking. Maybe it wasn't such a bad idea after all. Finally, against his better judgment, he signed up for the race. It would be one of the worst decisions as a dog musher that Leonhard Seppala ever made.

## CHAPTER 10

# Tragedy on the Trail

From the beginning, Leonhard didn't do any of the things necessary to properly prepare for the race. Usually mushers drove over the trail well in advance, putting in caches of dog food where they planned to rest. It also gave them a chance to figure out exactly where the trail was, where they might expect to encounter high winds, where the hard parts were, and where there was danger. But Leonhard had made his decision too late. He was so busy at work that he didn't have time to do any of those things. The best he could do was hire someone to go out and put in some food caches along the race trail.

On the morning of April 13, 1914, Leonhard and his dogs waited at the starting line out on the Bering Sea ice next to Nome. There were only three other teams. Leonhard's knees shook with excitement. He was about to compete against the best and most competitive sled dog racers in the world. At 9:00 am sharp, "Iron Man" John

Johnson started first with his 18 dogs, followed by Fred Ayer with 14 dogs, Leonhard and his 14 dogs, and last was Scotty Allan with 16 dogs.

Once they took off, Leonhard calmed down. The weather was good for the first 40 miles and then a blizzard set in. Visibility quickly dropped to near zero. From his map Leonhard knew they should be going north, so he took a compass reading and started up what he thought was Allen Creek. When Leonhard could no longer see the trail, he decided to let his lead dog, Suggen, choose the way and hope the dog would keep them on course. Suggen was the only dog in the team with any experience. He did his best but he had never been over this trail before. Somewhere in the storm Suggen got lost.

They came to the edge of a ravine. There was nothing but darkness and swirling snow ahead of them. The young dogs were panicking and desperate to escape the wind. They raced down the slope and quickly spotted a little cabin. The dogs headed straight for it, knocked the door down, and the entire team piled inside, taking Leonhard and the sled with them. In seconds the dogs managed to get themselves into a giant tangle of lines. After Leonhard got everyone calmed down and sorted out, he sat down on the sled to study the race map. There was no cabin anywhere around where they were supposed to be.

What a mess. They were stuck in a blizzard, there was no dog food, and Leonhard had no idea where they were. He decided that the only thing to do was head south until they found the Coastal Trail. He knew that trail and thought he could figure out from there where they were and how to get back to the race trail. When Leonhard tried to get the dogs to follow Suggen out into the storm, they refused. He pulled two dogs out, then two more. The first two turned around and shoved their way back inside the cabin. Everybody kept getting tangled up over and over. Leonhard had to straighten them out over and over. After a lot of shoving and shouting and cursing, he finally managed to drag everyone outside and slammed the door shut.

Luckily, when they climbed to the top of the ravine they felt a strong wind out of the north. The dogs were happy not to have the wind in their faces as they sped south. At the pace they were moving, Leonhard knew they would soon reach the Coastal Trail. He also knew that there were steep bluffs beside the trail that dropped off over 100 feet straight down to the sea ice below. The blowing snow made it impossible for him to see anything beyond Suggen. As they raced on, Leonhard grew more and more anxious.

Then, just when he needed it, there was a short lull in the wind. He could see that Suggen was just yards away from running over the edge of the bluff! Leonhard stomped on the foot-brake as hard as he could. But the snow on the slope was hard-packed and icy and he couldn't sink the brake into it. Leonhard kept a long, steel bar in the sled basket. He snatched it up. With all his might, he jammed it through a hole in the brake and into the snow. Everything jerked to a halt. The dogs kept tugging on their lines. With each jerk the steel bar was pulled farther and farther forward. Leonhard hung on to the bar with all his strength. If the bar came loose the dogs would run right over the edge of the bluff and fall to their deaths. "Suggen, come!" called Leonhard. Suggen couldn't hear Leonhard above the roaring wind. "Suggen! Come!" shouted Leonhard. This time Suggen heard the command. He turned around and tried to come to Leonhard, but the other dogs refused to turn and face into the wind. The steel bar was about to be pulled loose! Leonhard was terrified. The only way he could save himself was to let go and jump off the sled. But he couldn't do it. Somehow he had to save his dogs.

One more time. "Suggen! Come. Come!" Finally, the front four dogs turned into the wind and followed Suggen. "Keep coming! You can do it!" The other dogs refused to swing around. For a moment it looked as though everyone was going to swing back away from the wind. Leonhard refused to give up. "We're not gonna die here!"

Leonhard screamed. He clenched his teeth, grabbed the steel bar, and jerked it back with all his might. At the same time Suggen gave a mighty tug. Finally the rest of the team swung around.

The slope was icy and slippery. It was nearly impossible to climb up against the powerful wind. They kept trying. Climbing, slipping, climbing. Trying, trying, trying. Inch by inch by inch they climbed the slope until finally they reached the top.

Leonhard looked around and realized that somehow in the storm they had driven right over the Coastal Trail. After searching for a few minutes, Leonhard managed to find the trail. They went on to a little place called Bluff, several miles east of the race trail. There they got some badly needed rest. When the storm finally let up enough to travel, they sledded three hours through the dark to reach the checkpoint of Timber. The other three racers had been resting there and waiting out the storm for eight hours.

Four hours later everyone headed back out to continue the race. Leonhard drove his team to Council and then on to the checkpoint at Boston. He carefully examined his dogs. He could see they were exhausted. Several dogs had broken or missing toenails, some had cut pads, and a couple of dogs had slightly frozen flanks. Leonhard stood back and looked at the dogs. He knew he had failed in every way. Grief, sorrow, guilt; he felt all of that and more. He could not expect the dogs to go on. With a heavy heart, Leonhard withdrew his team from the race.

CHAPTER 11

# Getting It Right

In the 1914 All Alaska Sweepstakes Race, Leonhard had gone against his better judgment. He had made the terrible mistake of running dogs that were not properly trained and were too young and inexperienced for so difficult a race. Though he had done poorly, he wasn't about to give up.

Need determines success. Leonhard Seppala needed to prove that he could get a dog team through The Sweeps unharmed. More importantly, he needed to regain the trust of his dogs. They needed to believe that he would never hurt them again.

Leonhard pursued dog mushing with a new passion. In November 1914 he began taking his dogs out on easy, gentle training runs. The first day they ran just one mile, the next day two miles. Day by day he increased the distance. The dogs needed to get comfortable again with risk. So, as the runs grew longer, Leonhard ran them over trails they didn't know. Often they sledded over unbroken snow where they had to make their own trail. He ate with them, played with them, and took naps lying beside them on the snow. Over the winter Leonhard came to know everything about his dogs. He learned where each dog liked to run in the team. He figured out which dogs liked to run beside one another and which dogs didn't like each other. He learned how much rest they needed.

With all this time together, the dogs came to understand a lot about Leonhard. They knew by watching how he walked that he was going to put them in harness, or that he was going to feed them a big meal, or just hand out a snack. When he called a command, they learned by his tone of voice whether to speed up or slow down. By February 1915 Leonhard and his dogs could almost read each other's minds. Best of all, the dogs had once again learned to trust Leonhard.

When Leonhard announced that he was entering the 1915 Sweeps, no one thought he had a chance of winning. He got together with his good friend, Paul Kjegstad, who gave him lots of helpful advice. He told Leonhard where to rest along the route and where to stash food. He taught him about the strategy other racers used, particularly Scotty Allan, who had won The Sweeps three times. His brother, Asle, made Leonhard a new sled. It had longer runners, a shorter basket, and a brush bow on the front. Leonhard replaced his heavy leather harnesses with lightweight ones made of cotton webbing. He drove the team over the race trail so he and the dogs could become familiar with the geography. Constance helped him prepare and package dog food rations. Each ration consisted of raw hamburger frozen into chunks weighing 2 ½ to 3 ½ pounds. Leonhard scouted the race trail well ahead of time and buried the food in clean, two-gallon fuel oil cans where Paul had suggested.

## CHAPTER 12

# Queen Constance

As the time for the race got closer, a party atmosphere filled Nome. One day over dinner Constance announced, "Leonhard, I'm going to run for Sweepstakes Queen."

Leonhard was not the least bit surprised. "That's great! Wait until I tell the boys at the mines. Each vote sells for one cent so I bet you're gonna get a lot of votes from those guys. In fact, I bet you're gonna win!"

People began betting on who would be elected queen. As the bets got bigger and bigger, money poured in. Apparently there weren't many rules governing the voting process. Money came in from everywhere, even places outside of Alaska. When the officials began counting the votes, people milled around eagerly awaiting the results.

It was Constance by a landslide! Leonhard and the boys at the mines had come through. Constance received 102,430 votes while her nearest competitor got only 75,450 votes.

On race day Constance was driven to the starting line in a sled pulled by a team of beautiful huskies. The five race teams stood ready. The dogs were eager to run and kept lunging in their harnesses. Everyone was anxiously waiting for Constance to start the race. Playing it to the hilt, Constance smiled and waved to the crowd. Everybody cheered and waved back. In her hand she held a green and gold flag, the colors of the Nome Kennel Club. Constance tilted her head up in regal fashion. She slowly raised the flag over her head and quickly snapped it down.

It was a mass start! Five teams charged down the trail at the same time.

## CHAPTER 13

# The 1915 All Alaska Sweepstakes

The racers were Alex Holmsen, Paul Kjegstad, someone named John, Leonhard Seppala, and the musher most people thought would win, Scotty Allan.

There had been a lot of new snow, which made for a slow start. Leonhard was so keyed up that he wanted to jump off and run alongside the sled to speed them up. But his plan was to let them have their way in the beginning. So he sat down in the sled basket and enjoyed the ride.

All the teams were doing pretty well when Leonhard reached the Boston checkpoint, 106 miles from Nome. Scotty Allan had already arrived and was resting his dogs. The checkpoint was crowded with noisy spectators. Leonhard and his friend Paul knew the dogs wouldn't get much rest. They decided to sled six more miles to Fish River and set up a camp. Their plan was to rest there for six hours. After the dogs were fed, Paul and Leonhard went to work massaging the dog's muscles and tending their feet. While they rested, the other teams passed by.

Leonhard looked at Paul, "Do you think we should get going?"

"It's tempting but we need to stick to our plan. We said six hours here, so we stay six hours." Leonhard knew Paul was right so he settled back to rest.

The weather stayed nice as they moved past Telephone checkpoint and through Death Valley. By Gold Rush checkpoint, Leonhard and his dogs were in the lead. His team was running faster than Paul's team, so gradually they left him farther and farther behind. At Candle, the turnaround point, they were 204 miles into the race. Leonhard checked in and decided to head right back to Gold Run without resting. Somehow, before he left Candle, one of his dogs got loose. Race rules stated that a musher must finish with all the dogs he started with. Leonhard had no choice. He had to catch the dog. At first he tried to coax her to come to him, but all the noise and confusion had frightened the dog. She wouldn't let Leonhard get anywhere near her. Finally, Leonhard made a flying leap toward the dog and managed to tackle her. She was so startled, she bit Leonhard's hand. As luck would have it, a doctor was there and came to Leonhard's aid. With his hand bandaged and all the dogs back in the team, he took off for Gold Run, 28 miles back down the trail.

When he arrived at Gold Run, the checkpoint official asked, "How long are you planning to stay?"

"Six hours," replied Leonhard. He quickly fed the dogs so they could get some rest. While they dozed, he massaged their muscles and tended their feet. This didn't give Leonhard much time to rest. Finally he laid down on a bench and fell into a deep sleep. Later he was awakened when someone saw Scotty Allan's team approaching. By then they had been at Gold Run six hours as Leonhard had planned. The long rest had been good for the dogs and they were eager to go.

Just outside of Gold Run Leonhard looked back and saw Scotty Allan catching up. Even from a distance Leonhard could see that Scotty's team looked tired. Leonhard decided to play some mind games with him. Leonhard stepped lightly on the brake and called, "Easy". The dogs eased to a slow walk. As Scotty's team passed by, Leonhard looked a little downcast. He shook his head and said in a sad, weary voice, "My dogs are all in. I have no hope of winning."

Scotty waved and then urged his dogs to speed up. As he pulled ahead, Leonhard smiled. He knew Scotty now figured he was going to win. Scotty arrived at Boston checkpoint, 106 miles from Nome, and settled in for a good long rest. From there, he planned to travel straight through to Nome. When Leonhard arrived, he checked in and then headed right back out onto the trail. His plan was to continue from Boston to Council checkpoint where he would rest. Then he would drive the final 60 miles to Nome. When Scotty saw Leonhard sign in and then leave without resting, he panicked. Scotty quickly got his dogs up and took off after Leonhard. Scotty Allan, veteran dog driver, three time winner of the All Alaska Sweepstakes Race, had fallen for one of the oldest tricks in the book.

Any experienced long-distance dog musher can tell you that dogs know how to tell time. How they do that isn't really a mystery. Dogs watch their driver's every move. After a while they learn that certain movements tell them what to expect. Dogs are geniuses at this. When you stop for a six hour rest, they expect six hours rest. If they only get one hour, two hours, or whatever, they know they didn't get their full rest and they won't give you their best. In fact, they will sometimes just sit down and refuse to get up. So, you can bet that when Scotty got his dogs up early to chase after Leonhard's team, Scotty's dogs were not happy.

Leonhard and his team arrived in Council on Friday evening at about 7:15. After resting a little more than seven hours, Leonhard and his team took off on the final leg of the race. Scotty, who had followed Leonhard from Council, left twenty minutes later. At Timber, Leonhard could see Scotty chasing after him. Leonhard figured he had only about a four minute lead. At Topkok Mountain, fifty miles from Nome, Leonhard looked back. Scotty was nowhere to be seen. Leonhard wondered, *Has he somehow passed us?* Leonhard stood on the runners of his sled and looked over his team as they moved steadily along the trail. The dogs had been in fine condition at the start of the race and the long rests had helped them stay that way. Leonhard thought*, Don't worry. Stick to the plan. Just keep going.*

At Fort Davis, three miles from Nome, Leonhard heard the roar of cannons announcing his arrival as the winner. It was a glorious moment for Leonhard and his dogs. On Saturday, April 17, Leonhard Seppala and his team of 16 Siberian Huskies, all in harness, stepping high, looking happy and healthy, crossed the finish line. They had won the 1915 All Alaska Sweepstakes Race.

## CHAPTER 14

# Battle of Wills

Togo was probably born just a few days before Leonhard won the 1916 All Alaska Sweepstakes Race. Later that year Togo made his daring escape from the kennel. He ran through a storm and caught up with Leonhard and Mr. Stevenson as they headed for Dime Creek. Togo was only eight months old on that fateful November day when Leonhard put him in the team.

Over the winter of 1916—1917 Leonhard let Togo run beside lead dogs Russky, Suggen, Scotty, and Fritz. Togo paid attention and learned commands quickly. Leonhard knew that being a lead dog was stressful. He remembered his promise to use Togo carefully and sparingly. So he often rotated Togo back in the team where he could relax.

Since Togo had so much freedom as a puppy, it came as no surprise that this smart, determined, little dog had a mind of his own. In the beginning, this created problems between him and Leonhard. For example, one of the biggest frustrations for Leonhard was Togo's insistence that they travel in a straight line. The dog had an amazing sense of direction. Once he set out on a heading, Togo was determined to maintain a straight line no matter what. If they were traveling across open tundra or on a trail that was fairly straight, Togo was fine and there was no problem. But on frozen, winding rivers it was a different story.

One day they were following a route on an icy river toward one of the gold mines. Togo had been on the river once before, so he knew the trail. As they approached the first bend, Togo figured the obvious thing to do was jump up on the bank and cut straight across the land. After all, why go around a long bend when you can just keep going straight? It made perfect sense to Togo. Never mind that the bank was steep, clogged with soft, deep snow, and thick with brush. None of that mattered to Togo. Without warning he scrambled up the side of the bank and shoved himself headfirst into a tangle of willows. The bushes were so thick he couldn't move forward, he couldn't move left, and he couldn't move right. Togo was not a dog who gave up easily. He stood there belly deep in soft snow, searching for a way through the willows.

Meanwhile, Leonhard stood on the frozen river with a bewildered look on his face. "Togo, what are you doing?"

Togo turned his head and looked Leonhard straight in the eye. He cocked his head to one side as though he was wondering, *What do you think I'm doing?*

"Togo, get back down here."

Leonhard finally figured out that Togo was trying to go in a straight line across the land rather than go around the bend. "Togo, you knucklehead. You can't get through those willows. Get back down here right now!"

Togo took a deep breath and let out a sigh. He looked as though he was thinking, *If this guy had a brain in his head he would see I'm just trying to save us a few steps.* Frustrated and annoyed, Togo finally slid backwards down the bank. With his head held high, he led the team around the bend as though that's what he had planned all along.

During that first winter it was often a battle of wills between Togo and Leonhard. It wasn't easy for them to work out their differences. But Leonhard kept giving him plenty of opportunities to learn how to be a lead dog. Like all great leaders, Togo had to learn that the musher and lead dog are a team within the team. When he finally got this bit of wisdom into his stubborn brain, Togo got much better at following commands. In fact, he got so good that Togo became Leonhard's favorite lead dog.

In 1917 Leonhard again won the All Alaska Sweepstakes Race. It was his third straight win. Leonhard

Seppala was on his way to becoming a legend in his own time.

The year 1918 was eventful in many ways. Togo competed in his first race when he was chosen to be on Leonhard's team in the second running of the Borden Marathon. The race was 26 miles and 385 yards long, the same distance as a human marathon. Leonhard came in second behind musher Fred Ayer.

The United States and Germany were still at war. Most of Nome's young men left to join the military or look for better paying jobs in the Lower 48 states. The mining industry nearly shut down for lack of manpower. Luckily, Leonhard was able to keep his job. The 1918 All Alaska Sweepstakes Race was canceled. The prize money was donated to the Red Cross and some other war-related funds.

Besides war and the economy, there was an even worse threat that worried residents of Nome — Spanish Influenza. This horrible disease was killing millions of people as it moved around the entire world. On October 20, 1918, the ship *SS Victoria* brought the deadly virus to Nome. From there it spread across the Seward Peninsula, killing more than 200 Alaska Natives and at least 30 Caucasians. Also on board the *SS Victoria* were Constance and Leonhard's two year old niece, Sigrid Hallstrom.

In the early spring of 1918 Leonhard's younger sister, Felicie, who was living with her husband and daughter in Seattle, died from tuberculosis. As was the custom of the time, Leonhard and Constance took Sigrid into their home and raised her as their own child. Sigrid was a welcome addition to the family. The Seppalas had a yard full of puppies to play with which helped the little girl deal with her loss. She quickly settled into her new home.

The care and feeding of the dogs and maintaining equipment was hard work and took up a lot of time. But it wasn't all work and no play. On days off Leonhard often loaded Constance and Sigrid onto his sled and took them for a ride, just for fun. Sometimes Constance drove her own team with Sigrid in the basket. For the Seppalas, dogs and dog mushing was a happy, family affair.

Togo became Leonhard's main lead dog on all their major treks around the Seward Peninsula. In 1919 Leonhard and his team won first place in the Borden Cup Marathon. They won so many local races with Togo in lead that he soon became the most famous lead dog in Alaska. When Leonhard was asked why he thought they won so many races he said, "Because I use the dogs so much and they are always fit."

## CHAPTER 15

# A Job For Leonhard

Leonhard was now a supervisor at work. But there wasn't much going on at the gold mines, so Leonhard was looking for a way to make some extra income. Since the beginning of construction in 1915, the Alaska Railroad had been laying more and more tracks. The first tracks went north from Seward to Anchorage. Then, at the same time, tracks were laid north from Anchorage and south from Fairbanks. By late 1920 only 100 miles of track were needed to complete the entire route from Seward to Fairbanks. Leonhard saw an opportunity. He planned to spend three months during the coming winter of 1920—1921 shuttling supplies and people back and forth over the 100-mile gap.

Not everyone thought Leonhard's idea was a good one. Earlier in 1920 the Alaska Railroad Commission formally announced that Colonel John C. Gotwals had come to Alaska to assume his duties as president of the

Alaska Road Commission. Colonel Gotwals had strong opinions on how things should be done. He believed Caterpillar tractors should be used to haul supplies to construction sites because they were cheaper to run than teams of horses or dogs.

The first thing Colonel Gotwals did upon his arrival was to inspect local wagon trails and roads in the Anchorage area. Next, he decided to inspect trails that led to and from mines in the interior of Alaska. He was told that the only way to travel over the remote trails in winter was by dog sled. Colonel Gotwals wanted the best dog musher for the job, so of course Leonhard's name came up.

One day the phone rang at Leonhard's house. He was told to come down to the telegraph office to pick up a telegram. When he read the message, he raced home to talk with Constance.

"It looks like I won't be hauling freight between the railroad tracks after all."

"Oh? And why is that?" asked Constance.

"There's this guy, Colonel Gotwals, down in Anchorage. He runs the Alaska Road Commission and wants to inspect a bunch of trails in the Interior. He's got big plans. He wants to go around the Kuskokwim region, then over Rainy Pass, and around the foothills of Mount McKinley. He needs someone to drive him around by dog sled, so he asked me if I wanted the job."

"That's quite a trip he has planned," commented Constance. "Mount McKinley is the highest peak in Alaska and I hear it's beautiful. How long is this trip supposed to take?"

"He figures it'll take about three months. It's a pretty good deal. The job pays more than I could ever make hauling freight, plus I get to see a part of Alaska I've never been to before."

"It sounds like you've already decided to take the job," said Constance.

"Yup. I already sent a telegram back telling him that I accept his offer. I'm going to take 15 dogs and my big freight sled so there's room for the Colonel and all his stuff. I have to sled over to Manley Hot Springs and pick him up."

"Manley Hot Springs? How far is that?"

"About 650 miles."

"Oh, is that all," said Constance with a little laugh. "I know you'll be stopping at roadhouses where you can sleep and get something to eat. But I'll still fix some of your favorite trail food to take along."

This journey was such a big deal that the Nome Nugget newspaper ran a story describing their proposed journey. On December 30, 1920, Constance and Sigrid waved good-bye to Leonhard as he set out from home on his long adventure. Togo was in lead. It was a bit windy when they hit the Coastal Trail and the temperature was a little below zero. At that time of year the sun gives off very little heat so Leonhard knew it wouldn't get any warmer during the day. It didn't matter. Leonhard was toasty warm in his fur parka and boots and the dogs had thick coats to keep them warm.

They got off to a relaxed start. Leonhard and the dogs had been over the first couple of hundred miles so many times that Togo knew the route and Leonhard seldom had to give him commands. Leonhard loved sledding on the Seward Peninsula and settled back to enjoy the ride. The only sound was the slight grating of the sled runners gliding over the snow and the soft panting of the dogs. The air was so pure it had no smell. To his left were hills rolling endlessly over the horizon. Only the occasional bush stuck up here and there through the glistening, white snow. To his right lay sea ice, some flat, some broken, and some piled two or three feet high. With a lightly loaded sled, they made good time as they passed well-known places like Safety, Solomon, and Topkok. Those first few days were perfect. Leonhard felt as though nothing could go wrong.

In December the sun doesn't rise very high above the horizon and dawn to dusk is only about five hours.

Traveling mostly in the daylight, it only took a couple of days to reach Elim where they spent a comfortable night. They were now 123 miles from home.

The next morning Leonhard was up early to study the weather. He noted the wind was coming off Norton Sound from the southwest. He knew the on-shore wind meant that they could cross Norton Sound without worrying about the ice breaking up and carrying them out to sea. But he also knew very well that the on-shore wind would be shoving water under the sea ice toward land. The ice right along the shore is frozen to the land and is called shore-fast ice. Sea ice offshore floats freely over the ocean.

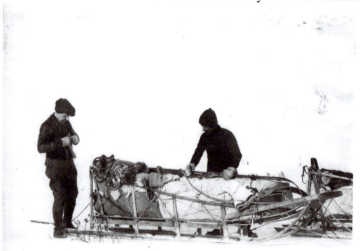

Sigrid Seppala Hanks Collection, Carrie M. McLain Memorial Museum

Example of the kind of freight sled Leonhard Seppala used on his 1921 expedition with Colonel Gotwals.

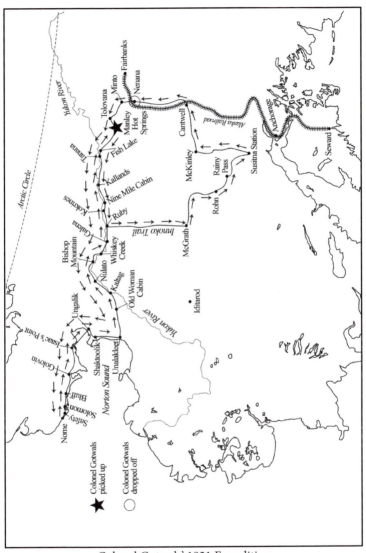

Colonel Gotwals' 1921 Expedition

When there is a strong wind coming in toward the land, the wind can cause water to rise so high that the shore-fast ice becomes completely covered by water. This can create a very dangerous situation because the water over the shore-fast ice can be so deep that a musher and dog team can't get off the ice.

After Leonhard and the dogs finished breakfast, Togo led the team out of Elim in the early morning light. They moved along the shore for about five miles and then crossed a bay eleven miles wide. They sledded silently passed an abandoned Eskimo village. From there it was easy traveling along a flat sand spit about four miles to Moses Point.

Leonhard called, "Whoa. Let's take a break." He handed out snacks to the dogs, ate some frozen cooked beans, and lay down on top of the sled for a short nap. When he woke up, Leonhard got off his sled and walked up to Togo. Like most mushers, Leonhard often talked out loud to his dogs. Somehow that made it easier to make decisions. He usually spoke to Togo as though he were a person and could understand everything Leonhard said.

He looked out over the ice. "The wind is still out of the southwest, Togo. The ice looks a little rough in places but I don't think we'll have any problems. It's an easy 15 miles across this part of the sound to Isaac's Roadhouse. Once we get there, we're finished for the day."

## CHAPTER 16

# Terror on the Ice

Togo had been here before and he knew very well what lay ahead. In the distance he could see a huge, rocky headland that jutted about a mile out into Norton Sound. Its steep sides thrust skyward almost 500 feet, making it look vaguely like a giant, bald head. In fact, just that year the name of this headland had been officially changed from Castle Rock to Bald Head. Regardless of what it was called, there was no place to cross because the sheer-sides were too steep to climb. Togo knew the route. He knew he had to lead the team across part of Norton Sound, turn right, head out onto the sea ice, guide them through rough ice, maybe swing around open water, go past Bald Head, turn left, and head back to shore. That was how they would get to Isaac's Roadhouse.

Togo needed to be able to move freely so he could find the way through rough ice. Leonhard lengthened his tug line and put him on a 12 foot lead. For a few minutes, the man and dog stood beside one another quietly looking out over the sea ice. Leonhard gave Togo's shoulders a quick pat and said, "Okay, Togo, let's get going."

Togo looked up at Leonhard, wagged his tail, and thought, *No problem, Boss. I'll get us there.* He watched Leonhard climbed back onto the sled. Then he gave a quick tug on his line and led the team out onto the ice of Norton Sound.

At first the ice was flat and they moved along at a good clip. About half a mile from shore they came to some rubble ice and Togo quickly found a way through. But it didn't last. Soon the ice was so jumbled and piled up that it looked as though a giant hand had grabbed the ice, crumpled it, and tossed it back down. Togo couldn't see where to go.

A good lead dog and musher have to work together. By now Togo was a very skilled lead dog and knew this. He stopped and looked back at Leonhard. Of course, Leonhard was taller than Togo and he could see a route. Togo listened as Leonhard called commands. "Haw" meant turn left and "Gee" meant turn right. Winding through the rubble and climbing up and over huge chunks of ice slowed them down, but together Leonhard and Togo got the team safely through the rough ice.

Just as they finally broke out onto flat ice, it started snowing. The wind picked up and Leonhard could hardly see Togo through the blowing snow. The sun was already low on the horizon. Leonhard trusted Togo to find the way but he called Togo to speed up anyway so they could reach the roadhouse before dark.

They were moving along at a pretty fast pace when the team suddenly slowed way down. Leonhard stuck his head forward, trying to peer through the blowing snow. He was shocked by what he saw. The dogs were nearly up to their bellies in what looked like slush! They were looking around as though they were confused and trying to figure out what to do.

"All right!" commanded Leonhard, "Let's go!"

Every time the dogs tried to move forward they sank into the slush a little deeper. The sled started filling up with water. The wheel dogs were thrashing frantically with their front feet trying to keep their noses above water. The wheel dogs were drowning!

Leonhard stepped off the sled runners and sank to his waist in slush! Water started pouring into his clothing. He was being pulled under! Instinctively, Leonhard grabbed the sled with both hands and heaved himself up on top of the sled bag. He watched in horror as water rose quickly up to his knees. Everything was happening so fast! He could feel himself starting to panic. Leonhard looked down at the dogs. Their eyes were wild with terror. Leonhard's mind was racing. *Is the ice breaking up? Think! Do something!*

"Togo!" Leonhard shouted. "Togo!"

He could barely make out Togo through the blowing snow. Togo's long lead had let him swim through the slush. Togo was standing on solid ice!

"Rrruff!" Togo barked.

Leonhard knew he had to reach Togo. He quickly stepped off the sled again and sank to his armpits. He could feel nothing under his feet! Leonhard seized the gangline and pulled himself forward. The dogs were in a panic, their eyes wide with fear. As Leonhard pulled himself past the dogs, they grabbed at his clothing with their teeth. They climbed onto his shoulders. They clawed at his head. Their weight was pushing Leonhard under water! Leonhard knew he had to rescue himself first if he was going to save the dogs. He kept pulling them off and shoving them away. His elbow slammed into a dog's face. He punched another with his fist. Leonhard was fighting for his life! "Get off!" he roared, "You're drowning me!"

Leonhard looked toward Togo. Togo scratched frantically at the ice with his front paws.

"Rrruff! Rrruff!"

It was as though Leonhard could see the words in Togo's eyes — *Keep coming! Keep coming!* His hands were so cold, he couldn't feel them anymore. His entire body was going numb. Leonhard willed his hands to grip the line and pulled. When he finally reached Togo, he was so cold he could barely move. Somehow Leonhard found the strength to climb up onto the ice and collapsed.

Togo turned his attention to the dogs. He kept lunging and straining with his tug line, trying to pull the dogs forward. He barked sharply, over and over, as though ordering the dogs to pull.

Cold as he was, Leonhard managed to get up and grab hold of Togo's tug line. Together they slowly dragged the dogs toward solid ice. Togo kept pulling forward as Leonhard grabbed the first dog by its collar, then the next and the next. One by one, Leonhard dragged them up onto the ice. Finally, they had all the dogs out of the water except the two wheel dogs who were completely submerged.

"Rrruff!" Togo barked sharply, commanding the dogs to pull. Everyone strained against their harness. Leonhard reached down into the water, grabbed the collar of one of the wheel dogs, and dragged it up onto the ice. Then the second. The dogs appeared dead as they lay motionless on the ice. Leonhard could not stop to help them. The sled was completely under water and sinking fast. It was so heavy that it was starting to drag them backwards. If it dragged them back into the water, they would all drown!

Again, Leonhard reached into the icy water. His hands were numb but he willed them to grasp the front of the sled. "Togo, pull!" Togo gave a mighty tug. All the dogs lunged forward. The sled broke the surface of the water and edged part way up onto the ice. It was unbelievably heavy. The dogs' feet started slipping backwards on the slick ice. Leonhard couldn't hold on much longer!

Leonhard yelled, "Pull, Togo! Pull!"

"Rrruff! **Rrruff!**" Togo barked. The dogs dug their toenails into the ice. They strained and pulled as hard as they could. Leonhard gave it everything he had. Inch by inch by inch, together they pulled the sled up onto the ice.

Everyone stood silent, chests heaving, out of breath, and exhausted. Then, as if by a miracle, the wheel dogs staggered to their feet, shook themselves off, and looked around as though coming out of a dream. Leonhard looked at them in disbelief. He looked over at Togo who was staring at the wheel dogs.

"Rrrrrruff!" Togo bounced up and down and spun around in a dance of pure happiness. The other dogs joined in and soon they were all bouncing around, barking, and howling. Everyone was alive! A big smile spread across Leonhard's face. Then, overcome with emotion, he bowed his head and tears of joy ran down his cheeks.

But they couldn't dally. They were all soaked and they were starting to freeze. Working would generate body heat and the dogs' coats would quickly dry out. Leonhard too was soaked but he would just have to put up with being cold and miserable. Leonhard climbed onto the sled and Togo started them towards shore. About an hour later Leonhard stopped the team and stood staring in disbelief. The wind had driven the water up onto shore. It was so deep, there was no way they could get off the ice.

"Togo, come haw," called Leonhard. Togo turned the team around to the left and headed away from shore. After a few minutes Leonhard called, "Togo, gee". They turned right and sledded over to Bald Head. At the bottom of a steep bluff Leonhard saw a place where they could get off the ice and onto a rocky beach. It was too narrow for the sled so Leonhard turned Togo loose so he could scamper to shore and show the other dogs where to go. He left the sled on the ice and Togo lead them along the beach for two hours until they finally reached Isaac's Roadhouse.

Togo and his team were put in the kennel and rewarded with a huge meal of salmon and tallow. Leonhard stood watching the dogs wolf down every morsel. As Togo licked his paws clean, Leonhard smiled and marveled at what an amazing dog he was. Togo looked up at Leonhard and once again their eyes met. Leonhard kneeled down and put his arm around Togo's shoulders. In a soft voice Leonhard said, "We're alive because of you, Togo." Togo swished his tail and laid his head on Leonhard's shoulder. For a long time they stayed like that … silent … breathing.

## CHAPTER 17

# Exploring Interior Alaska

The next day Leonhard was relieved to see that the wind had stopped blowing toward shore and the high water had taken itself back out to sea. Togo easily guided everyone back to the sled, which was resting on the ice within easy reach. Leonhard hooked up the team and Togo led them back to the roadhouse so Leonhard could dry out the rest of his gear.

The following morning they set out at first light. This time their trek across Norton Sound was uneventful. After about 85 miles, they reached the village of Unalakleet. From there they crossed the 90 mile-long Kaltag Portage to the Yukon River. At Kaltag they turned north and followed the Yukon River for more than 250 miles to the Tanana River. Then they sledded 54 miles along the Tanana to Manley Hot Springs. There, on day 25 of their journey, they met Colonel John C. Gotwals.

After a brief rest, and with the Colonel settled snuggly in the sled basket, they traveled about 170 miles back down the Tanana and Yukon rivers to the village of Ruby. From there they turned south along the famous Innoko Trail. They were now headed straight into the heart of gold mining country. This was new territory for Togo and the other dogs. It was also new to Leonhard and he was excited to see it. With Togo in single lead, they traveled past low-lying hills, along narrow creeks, and around countless bends and turns.

One day Colonel Gotwals commented, "Your lead dog keeps a good pace. And he stays right on the trail."

Leonhard laughed, "That's because he doesn't know where he's going."

The Colonel looked back at Leonhard with a quizzical look but didn't ask any questions. After about 160 miles, they reached the bustling village of Innoko. There were a few low mountains, but mostly the land was rolling hills and wide valleys, some forested, some not. A seemingly infinite number of creeks and rivers meandered across the vast snow-covered land. There were trails everywhere, sometimes five or six leading to and from a village, all heading toward goldmines scattered across the region. Out there in the wilderness were hundreds, if not thousands, of men working the mines, each one hoping to find riches buried beneath the frozen land.

At Innoko and McGrath the Colonel spoke with local people. For several days they made side trips to mines in the area. On almost every trip, Togo ran in single lead. When the inspections were over, they started back to McGrath.

By now Togo had led them to and from McGrath so many times that he knew exactly where he was and where he was headed. So, of course, it seemed perfectly logical to him to shorten the route. The first bend in the trail went to the left. Togo knew this. So he jumped left off the trail and climbed up the bank. Of course he ran smack into deep snow and dense brush.

"What is that dog doing?" demanded Colonel Gotwals.

"Togo's up to his old shenanigans," replied Leonhard. "He knows where he's going now and he thinks it would be better to go straight across the land instead of going around the bend. Don't worry, Colonel, I'll get him back on the trail."

"Togo, come down here. You know you can't get through that brush."

Dogs can feel embarrassed and they certainly can be stubborn. So, to save face, Togo stood on top of the bank looking off into the brush as if he was thinking, *Just a minute boss. I think I see a way through.*

"Togo, you knucklehead, get back down on this trail!" Leonhard bellowed.

Togo had learned a long time ago that when Leonhard called him a knucklehead, it was time to follow orders. In a single bound, Togo leaped down off the bank.

Sigrid Seppala Hanks Collection, Carrie M. McLain Memorial Museum

Togo in single lead on the Colonel Gotwals' Expedition, March 13, 1921

With his head held high, he yanked on his tug line, and led the team around the bend.

"If this was the army, that dog would be given some tough discipline," said Colonel Gotwals.

Leonhard's eyebrows shot up in surprise. This was his team, the dogs were working hard, and he wasn't interested in any criticism from the Colonel.

"Well, Colonel, this isn't the army."

## CHAPTER 18

# The First Alaskan Relay

While in McGrath, Leonhard heard about a man who was in serious need of a doctor over in the gold mining town of Iditarod, about 120 miles away. In such a remote location there were no doctors, so word was sent to Anchorage requesting a doctor be sent to Iditarod.

Just the previous year Dr. John Beeson had been hired by the Alaska Railroad Hospital in Anchorage for the positions of Chief of Staff and Chief Surgeon. He had little wilderness experience. Nevertheless, arrangements were immediately made to send him to Iditarod. On January 24, 1921, Dr. Beeson traveled by train to Nenana. From there a relay of seven mushers, traveling day and night, delivered him to Iditarod. The entire journey from Anchorage to Iditarod was a little more than 500 miles and took five days and ten hours. For the times, this was amazingly fast.

Dr. Beeson did what he could for the man and started back to Anchorage by dog team. A few days later

Leonhard and Colonel Gotwals finished their work in the McGrath area. They headed east to inspect more trails around the foothills of Mount McKinley. With Togo in lead, they quickly caught up with the doctor's team. Together they crossed a vast 80 mile stretch of rolling hills, open windswept tundra, and dense forest until they reached the South Fork of the Kuskokwim River. From there they sledded down the river about 20 miles to the Rohn Roadhouse where they spent the night.

The following morning they left the South Fork and traveled a few miles along the Tatina River. After about seven miles Leonhard called, "Gee, Togo, gee!" Togo swung smartly to the right and entered the Dalzell Gorge. A frozen creek crowded with brush provided a narrow, icy trail. Togo and Leonhard had never traveled this route before. Even though Leonhard had been warned that it was difficult and dangerous, he had no idea what they were up against.

Togo moved swiftly along the trail. Suddenly there was a loud *crack!* Togo felt a little shudder under his feet. He stopped and stood perfectly still. Leonhard urged him forward but he refused to move. Togo looked back at Leonhard, his eyes wide and unblinking, as if he was thinking, *Something is wrong here.*

Everything looked fine to Leonhard. "Togo! Let's go!"

Togo slowly moved his left front foot forward and pressed gently down on the trail.

## *Crack!*

Togo vanished through a gaping hole in the ice! Leonhard jammed on the brake. The dogs pulled back trying desperately to keep from being dragged into the hole. Leonhard grabbed his iron bar and jammed it through the brake and into the ice. The sled could not go forward as long as the bar held. Leonhard ran forward and dropped to his knees beside the hole. He could see Togo lying on his side on the creek bed about four feet below. The drivers behind Leonhard's team ran up to see what had happened.

Togo stood up and shook himself off. He looked up at Leonhard.

"Rrruff!"

"Would you look at that!" exclaimed Leonhard. "This whole creek has dried up under the trail. We've been traveling on nothing more than a thin shell of ice."

"Rrruufff! Rrruufff!"

Everyone laughed. One of the men said, "I think Togo wants out of there."

Togo couldn't climb out on his own, so Leonhard carefully lowered himself through the narrow hole. Leonhard was a strong guy but he wasn't very tall. He put his hands under Togo's belly and heaved him up over his head. One of the men grabbed Togo by the collar and pulled him up. Leonhard climbed out and looked at Togo. He raised his eyebrows, shook his head, and said with a sigh, "I should have listened to you, Togo. You knew something wasn't right."

Togo cocked his head to one side as if he was thinking, *Yup, you got that right.*

The drivers stood around talking, trying to decide what to do. There really wasn't much to decide. The gorge was narrow and so clogged with brush that turning around was nearly impossible. Besides, they didn't know any other route. The only thing they could do was move forward and try to be careful. Many times that day the sound of cracking ice echoed through the gorge. Sometimes an entire team, sled and driver fell through; other times only a few dogs dropped out of sight. Several times Togo's team made it over thin ice only to hear the clatter of the team behind them breaking through.

After a few miles, the trail edged to the right and away from the creek. From there they climbed steeply up to Rainy Pass. They were now on the southern slope of the Alaska Range where they faced a new challenge. The mountains were known for being the heaviest snow-belt in all of Alaska. The men took turns skiing or snowshoeing ahead to cut a path while the dogs waded through belly-deep snow. Togo was the shortest dog and struggled the most, but he never gave up and worked as hard as he could.

Eventually, they hit the Skwentna River and the beautiful, wide trail that led straight down river and through a few miles of forested land to the Susitna River. They pulled up to the Susitna Roadhouse where they planned on taking a long rest. But Dr. Beeson was not interested in resting. Word had been sent up the trail that he was needed by his patients back at the hospital in Anchorage, so he wanted to head out right away.

Colonel Gotwals spoke to Leonhard. "Your team is in better shape than Dr. Beeson's so I think you should take him in to Anchorage so he can get back to the hospital."

Leonhard looked at his dogs. They had just been fed and everyone including Togo was curled up sound asleep. Leonhard understood that Dr. Beeson needed to get back to his patients but he also knew that the dogs were worn out. He spoke firmly to Colonel Gotwals, "The dogs are going to get some rest first and then we'll go."

A couple of hours later Leonhard woke Togo up. "Believe it or not, Togo, we have to travel." Togo looked up at Leonhard, a little blurry-eyed. He took a deep breath, stood up, stretched, yawned, and shook the sleep from his tired brain. Leonhard gently slipped Togo's harness on and scratched him behind his ears. When all the dogs were hooked up and ready to go, a weary Dr. Beeson plopped down in the sled.

Leonhard called "All right!"

Togo gave a tug. Nothing happened. The other dogs stood with their heads hanging down and swaying slightly, still half asleep. As usual Togo had more energy than any three dogs. He expected everyone to work no matter how tired they were. Leonhard stood silently on the runners, waiting. He knew exactly what was going to happen next.

Togo spun around in his harness. **"Rrrrrruff!!!"**

Every dog's head snapped up. Togo had spoken. The team leaned into their harnesses and off they went down the trail. Leonhard stood proudly on the runners with a big grin on his face. *Togo,* he thought to himself, *I can always count on Togo.*

When they arrived on the outskirts of Anchorage, Dr. Beeson gave Leonhard directions to the hospital. In 1921 Anchorage was a small town of fewer than 1,900 people, so it didn't take long for Togo to lead the team to the front door of the four-story building. Dr. Beeson thanked Leonhard and hurried inside. Togo expertly turned the team around and guided them out of town and back onto the trail. So concluded the first relay in Alaska.

## CHAPTER 19

# Chasing a Train

Leonhard returned to the Susitna Roadhouse and picked up Colonel Gotwals. They completed inspecting the trails among the foothills of Mount McKinley and then drove east through deep snow for two exhausting weeks. When they finally reached the railroad, the dogs were worn to a frazzle. Leonhard decided to make arrangements for them to ride on a flatcar up to the village of Nenana.

Leonhard got the sled up onto the flatcar but he couldn't find any place to secure the dogs. They had never ridden on a train before and he was worried that the dogs might leap off when it started moving. He found the brakeman and, after explaining the situation, asked, "Is there some way to secure the dogs?"

The brakeman looked at Leonhard and replied in a surly voice, "I couldn't care less if they jump off. Just get those dogs on that flatcar!"

Leonhard persisted, "First I need to be sure there's some way of securing them."

"There's no time for arguing. Hurry up and get that outfit on."

Leonhard was usually polite and not prone to anger. But to treat his dogs with such disrespect, to show such lack of concern for their safety, after all they had been through, all the miles they had pulled a sled, after hauling Dr. Beeson to Anchorage, and now this character doesn't care what happens to them??? Leonhard flew into a rage! He grabbed the sled and jerked it off the flatbed.

The brakeman looked shocked and then apologized. "I'm sorry. I'll help you get the dogs up there and we'll figure out how to tie them down."

"Get out of my way," shouted Leonhard. "I'm not interested in any apology from you."

Leonhard walked over to Togo and then, almost as an afterthought, spun around to face the brakeman. His eyes narrowed and he sneered, "For your information, these dogs can pull a sled as fast as your train can drive down those tracks!"

Leonhard didn't know if that was true, but then he really didn't care. Just as he finished harnessing the last dog, steam shot out from both sides of the engine. The dogs startled and jerked back. Leonhard grabbed the gangline to help Togo steady the team. "It's okay," said Leonhard. The train started slowly moving down the track - chug, chug,

chug. A huge cloud of black smoke belched into the sky just as the whistle blasted woo-wooo. The dogs were bug-eyed as this strange contraption started moving. Just as the last car passed by, the dogs caught a glimpse of Colonel Gotwals standing on the rear platform looking at them. The sight of their friend and the thought of chasing after the train was too much. The dogs suddenly forgot how tired they were and started racing down the tracks.

The train began picking up speed. The dogs began picking up speed. The train went faster. The dogs went faster. No matter how fast the train went, the dogs went just as fast. Two hours later Togo led the team into Nenana right alongside the train. When the brakeman jumped down off the train and saw Leonhard and his team standing there, he did a double-take. His eyebrows shot up and his jaw dropped down. He could hardly believe his eyes. There stood Leonhard Seppala beside his sled along with 15 dogs, heads held high, and tongues lolling out the sides of their mouths. Togo looked straight at the brakeman with a big smile and wagged his tail as if he was thinking, *Chasing this thing down the tracks was a lot of fun.*

The man shook his head in disbelief and muttered something under his breath.

Leonhard watched as he walked away. "Togo, I don't know what that guy just said, but I do believe he's got a lot more respect for you dogs now."

After resting a few days, Leonhard and the dogs made the 674 mile journey back to Nome. All totaled on this expedition, they had traveled over 3,000 miles.

## CHAPTER 20

# The Pupmobile

Back home winter soon turned to summer. Togo continued leading the team, only now they pulled what Leonhard called the pupmobile. The pupmobile was a wagon with wheels set to ride on an abandoned narrow-gauge railroad track. All summer long the dogs pulled the pupmobile loaded with supplies and people back and forth from Nome to the gold mines. Life was good. The dogs had lots of rest between trips and pulling a wagon along a railroad track was always more fun than hanging around the kennel being bored. The dogs had a purpose. They were well fed and well treated. At the end of the day each dog slept the night away in its own spacious doghouse next to the Seppala's home.

During the summer, dogs were still a family affair. Five year old Sigrid played with the puppies and helped socialize them. Sometimes Constance would pack a picnic lunch, Leonhard would turn five or six dogs loose, and they would all go fishing together.

For the next four years, Togo and the team continued hauling supplies along the trails during the winter and pulling the pupmobile during the summer. They also competed in quite a few local sled dog races. In 1923 Leonhard and his team easily won the popular Borden Cup Marathon. In fact, with Togo in lead, Leonhard won so many races that he was considered the best dog musher in Alaska and Togo the best lead dog.

Sigrid Seppala Hanks Collection, Carrie M. McLain Memorial Museum

The pupmobile. During the summer months, sled dogs were used to haul passengers and supplies to the gold mines along a narrow gauge railroad track.

Sigrid Seppala Hanks Collection, Carrie M. McLain Memorial Museum

While pulling the pupmobile, sled dogs were given lots of rest between trips. Togo is seen here with his front legs crossed.

## CHAPTER 21

# Trouble in Nome

Sigrid Seppala Hanks Collection, Carrie M. McLain Memorial Museum

Togo standing on a post with Leonhard Seppala.

The Pioneer Mining Company that Leonhard worked for had been sold in 1922 and was now called the Hammon Consolidated Gold Fields. It was run by Mark Summers. By 1924 the big gold rush was over and gold mining was seldom done by individual prospectors. Mostly only big companies with huge, expensive dredges mined for gold which was found ever deeper in the earth.

Nome had shrunk in population from over 20,000 people to fewer than 1,500. The town was divided into two separate parts. There was the Sandspit, a narrow strip of land west of Nome between the Bering Sea and the Snake River. That was where mostly Native people lived. On the other side of the Snake River was the central part of town, populated mostly by white people. Though it was small, Nome had grown up in many ways. It had a fine school and the 25-bed Maynard Columbus Hospital run by Dr. Curtis Welch with the aid of three nurses, Emily Morgan, Bertha Saville, and Anna Carlson.

In the fall of 1924 the temperatures around Alaska began dropping lower and lower. By November, the last ship had sailed south and fall quickly gave way to winter. There would be no more ships until spring. Nome was now isolated from the rest of the world by the frozen sea. No one had any reason to suspect what the future held.

On New Year's Day, 1925, Nurse Emily Morgan was called to the Sandspit to see a sick five year old Native

University of Alaska Fairbanks Archive, Leonhard Seppala Collection
Nome was divided into two sections by the Snake River.
To the left is what was called the Sandspit and to the
right is the main part of town.

girl. Nurse Morgan reported to Dr. Welch that she believed
the girl had a severe case of tonsillitis. The following
day Dr. Welch was called to examine the girl but she had
already died. The little girl's mother was overcome with
grief and refused to allow him to examine the body.

There followed an unusual number of sick children
diagnosed with tonsillitis. On January 11, Dr. Welch
examined a six year old boy who was thought to have a
severe case of tonsillitis and admitted him to the hospital.
Dr. Welch discussed the patient with his nursing staff. It
was during this discussion that Nurse Morgan suggested
that the boy might have diphtheria. Years ago she had
diphtheria and recognized the signs and symptoms - fever,

difficulty breathing, and a membrane that lined the throat. When he examined the boy again, Dr. Welch saw that he had developed the tell-tale membrane and concluded that Nurse Morgan was right. There was a small amount of diphtheria antitoxin stored at the hospital but it was six years old. Dr. Welch had no idea if it would do any good or if it might even do harm, so he decided not to give it to the boy. Late on January 20, the boy died.

Dr. Welch realized he had an epidemic on his hands. He asked Nome's Mayor, George Maynard, to meet with him early the next morning. But before he had even gotten out of bed on January 21, Dr. Welch was called to see a six-year old Native girl. He diagnosed her as having diphtheria. There was no time to waste. Dr. Welch and Nurse Morgan went straight to the mayor's office to report what was happening.

After hearing what they had to say, Mayor Maynard summoned the members of the Nome City Council for an emergency meeting. They decided to establish a quarantine. The schools, churches, movie theaters, and lodges were ordered closed. Public gatherings were forbidden. Dr. Welch knew this was only the first step. He made it clear that the only way to stop a full-blown epidemic was to get more serum and get it fast. First they needed to find out if there was any serum in Alaska and, if so, where. As soon as the meeting was over, Dr. Welch hurried over to the office of the U.S. Army Signal Corps. He requested messages be sent to Fairbanks, Juneau, and Anchorage, the three biggest communities in Alaska, and ask if they had any serum.

Nurses Morgan and Saville began the daunting task of visiting as many homes as possible, alerting the residents to stay home. They posted a quarantine sign on the front door of any home where a person was suspected of having diphtheria. No one was allowed to enter or leave those homes.

On January 23, Mayor Maynard telegraphed Dan Sutherland, Alaska's delegate to Congress in Washington, DC, asking for help in getting serum sent to Nome.

On January 24, the Nome City Council formed a Board of Health to formally deal with the epidemic. They asked Mark Summers, president of Hammon Consolidated Gold Fields, to be the chairman. He accepted the position.

As word of the epidemic spread, people began sending messages to Governor Bone in Juneau, the capital of Alaska. Everyone was telling him how to get serum to Nome before anyone even knew if there was any in the State.

In the meantime, on January 26, Dr. Beeson at the Alaska Railroad Hospital in Anchorage, discovered he had 300,000 units of diphtheria antitoxin at his hospital.

This was the same Dr. Beeson whom Leonhard Seppala had helped back in 1921. Dr. Beeson immediately notified Governor Bone, Mayor Maynard, and Dr. Welch of his discovery.

Everyone on the Board of Health agreed that the fastest way to get the serum to Nome was to first bring it north from Anchorage by train.

Then what?

There began a huge debate over how to get the serum the rest of the way to Nome. Mayor Maynard wanted the serum shipped by train to Fairbanks where it would be loaded onto a plane and flown to Nome. This was a very daring plan. In 1925 airplanes were flown by pilots sitting in open cockpits with no protection from the weather. The few planes in Alaska were flown only during the warm, summer months. It was unlikely that a pilot could even survive flying in winter with temperatures of -50°F or even -60°F. Not only that, the planes in Fairbanks had already been disassembled and placed in storage for the winter.

Mark Summers thought the mayor's plan was reckless and said as much. He believed that transporting the serum by dog team was the only sure way of getting it to Nome. He recommended the serum be brought to the village of Nenana, the closest place on the railroad to Nome. From there it would be carried to Nome by dog team. The distance from Nenana to Nome was 674 miles. There was already a well-established mail trail that ran through a series of villages from Nenana to Nome. A mail driver would pick up the mail in one village, transport it by dog sled to the next village where he would hand it off to the next mail driver. Each man was responsible for a certain segment of the route, usually 100-150 miles in length and serving more than one village. The men who were employed to carry the mail were tough, seasoned dog mushers. As fast as they were, it still took about 25 days for the mail to reach Nome.

Mayor Maynard argued that 25 days was too long. He still thought using an airplane was better.

Summers proposed an idea that he thought would speed up delivery. The serum would first be taken by train to Nenana. From there one musher, carrying only the serum and no mail, would travel 319 miles west from Nenana to the village of Nulato. Another team would leave Nome at the same time and travel 355 miles east to Nulato. When the teams met, the musher from Nome would take possession of the serum, turn around, and sled back to Nome.

## CHAPTER 22

# Decision

Governor Bone was being pressured to do something. He sent another message to Alaska delegate Dan Sutherland demanding he get the U.S. Public Health Service involved. The Service quickly located 1.1 million units of serum in cities on the west coast of the United States. They agreed to ship it to Seattle, Washington as soon as possible. From there it would go to the ice-free port of Seward, Alaska and then north by train. The next available ship was the *Alameda*, due to arrive in Seattle on January 31. From there it would take the ship at least six days to reach Seward. That was encouraging, but they still had to figure out how to get the serum to Nome.

Mark Summers knew that if the Governor went with dog teams, the best team up to the task from Nome was Leonhard Seppala and his lead dog, Togo. It was like asking him to mush from Los Angeles, California to Phoenix, Arizona and back. He knew Leonhard would need time to prepare so he hurried to Leonhard's house. After telling him of the situation, he asked Leonhard, "Would you be willing to drive your team to Nulato and back?"

Without hesitating, Leonhard replied, "If you have that much faith in me and that is what's needed, I'll do it."

Summers pointed out, "The Governor might still choose to send the serum by plane. I'll let you know as soon as we know his decision."

As Summers was leaving, Leonhard said, "We haven't had a lot of snow to run on this year, so the dogs aren't as fit as usual. I'm not going to wait for a decision. We're going to start training right now."

Leonhard got his equipment out and began training his fastest and strongest dogs. Constance began preparing food for the journey. Over dinner that evening Leonhard told Constance he had formed a plan. "I'm going to start with 20 dogs. I'll drop dogs off in pairs at roadhouses or with locals along the way. When I reach Nulato, there'll be eight dogs left in the team. Then on the way back, I'll exchange tired dogs for rested ones so we can keep traveling as fast as possible."

"When you drop dogs off on the return trip, how will you get them back?"

"They'll have to stay where they get dropped off until the epidemic is over. After that I'll go get them or maybe some of those people will bring them home to us."

The media of the day - Associated Press, United Press, International News Service, and radio - quickly got hold of the story. A small town in Alaska cut off from the world by sea ice for the winter, was faced with a deadly epidemic. This was big news! Almost overnight, everyone in America and soon most of the people around the world knew about Nome's plight.

The battle over which way to transport the serum became heated. Mayor Maynard and others continued sending a stream of messages to Governor Bone trying to convince him that flying was the best choice. Mark Summers remained adamant - dogs not planes.

In Nome the situation continued to worsen. Dr. Welch instructed his nurses to keep visiting homes around Nome and the Sandspit to check for anyone showing signs of diphtheria. They reported there were now an additional 22 diagnosed cases, 30 more were suspected, and at least 50 other people were known to have been exposed to the deadly bacteria. The death toll from diphtheria now stood at five. A decision was needed.

Governor Bone decided to put his trust in dogs.

The Governor authorized Dr. Beeson to put the serum on the train in Anchorage and ship it to Nenana. Late on January 26, Dr. Beeson carefully wrapped the bottles containing the serum in a heavy quilt and secured it with rope. He hurried to the train station and handed the 20-pound bundle over to conductor Frank Knight. Within minutes the serum began its journey north to Nenana.

Time mattered. As the serum was heading north on the train, a new plan was made to speed the delivery. Instead of one team going all the way from Nenana to Nulato, a series of teams would be stationed along the route, forming a relay. Mail drivers would carry the serum by dog sled from one village to the next village. They would not carry any mail, just the serum. At each point the serum would be brought inside and warmed. Then it would be carried to the next village and the next and the next. Most of the mail drivers were Native Alaskans who had grown up in the Alaskan interior. These men were as tough as they come. They knew every inch of their routes. They would travel non-stop, no matter what the conditions. The Northern Commercial Company, who employed the mail drivers, quickly located their best and fastest men and sent them to their positions along the route.

# CHAPTER 23

# The Relay Begins

Late on January 27, 1925, as the train neared Nenana, Wild Bill Shannon eagerly awaited the serum's arrival. Wild Bill thrived on challenge. He was a prospector, a trapper, and one of the fastest mail drivers. Because Wild Bill was based in Nenana he had been chosen to make the first run in the serum relay.

As the train rumbled into Nenana, Wild Bill's nine dogs were already harnessed and ready to go. Conductor Frank Knight handed Wild Bill the 20-pound bundle and said, "Here's the serum."

Dr. Beeson had sent a letter with instructions on how to care for the serum. Wild Bill tied the bundle snuggly to the sled and then quickly read over the instructions. It clearly stated that the serum should not be allowed to freeze. Wild Bill glanced at the thermometer on the outside of the train station. It was 40 degrees below zero.

Normally when it was that cold Wild Bill would wait for daylight so the sun could warm the air and he could see the trail better. But Wild Bill knew people in Nome were counting on him and his dogs to get the serum to them as quickly as possible. He jammed the letter into his pocket, lifted the snowhook, and headed off into the night.

The first leg of the relay was 30 miles from Nenana to Minto. At first they followed the trail leading out of the village that ran beside the Tanana River. The trail was full of ruts and holes made by horses used to haul freight sleds. The only light was from a sliver of moon in a clear sky. The dogs couldn't see well in the dim light and kept stepping in holes. As they tripped and stumbled, their speed dropped to a slow walk. Wild Bill knew his dogs were going to get injured if they didn't get off the trail. He eased them down onto the frozen river and the dogs quickly picked up their pace.

Cold air sinks into low places like riverbeds. With every breath Wild Bill felt a stinging sensation on his nose and cheeks. He knew from experience that meant the temperature had fallen to around 50 degrees below zero. It is not true that breathing cold air will freeze the lungs of a dog or a man. If that were true, lips would freeze first, then the tongue, then the throat. That does not happen.

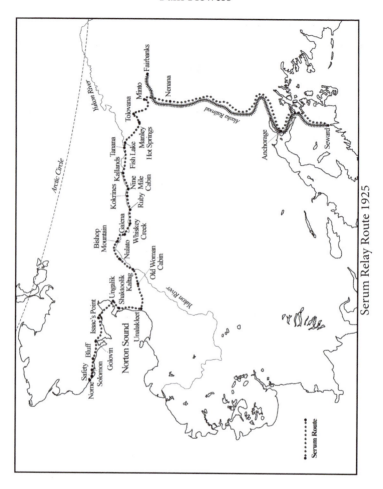

Serum Relay Route 1925

But breathing cold air does make a body work harder to stay warm and the extra work will quickly sap a body's energy. After about an hour Wild Bill noticed the dogs were running with their heads down close to the ice. He knew this was a sign that they were getting very tired, so he slowed the team to conserve their energy.

Wild Bill was beginning to have his own problems with the cold. His fingers were stinging and he knew that meant he wasn't getting enough blood circulating through them. He needed to get the warm blood that was deep inside his body to circulate into his fingers to warm them up. Otherwise his fingers would get frostbitten. He swung first one arm then the other in wide circles trying to move more blood into his fingers. At first this helped. But after a few minutes it wasn't enough, so he jumped off the sled and ran along side. He hoped making his body work harder would generate more heat. Wild Bill could feel himself warming up a bit. But after just a few minutes he was too tired to keep running, so he jumped back onto the sled runners. His hands felt like clubs and parts of his face had lost all feeling. Wild Bill knew he was becoming hypothermic, a state where the body gets so cold it slowly shuts down and finally dies. He wanted so badly to stop and rest. If only he could rest…..

At about three o'clock in the morning Wild Bill stumbled through the doorway of Campbell's Roadhouse. They had made it to Minto. The proprietor, Johnny Campbell, was used to seeing what happens to people when they travel in extreme cold. He knew exactly what to do. He took hold of Wild Bill's arm and helped him over to the wood stove and told him, "Sit here. Drink this hot coffee while I take care of the dogs." When Johnny went outside, he saw that all nine dogs were tired but four of them were so exhausted they could barely stand. Johnny unhooked the dogs and gently led them over to a lean-to. He fed them and then went back inside to check on Wild Bill.

Wild Bill asked, "Johnny, what's the temperature?"

"Sixty-two below."

Wild Bill asked, "Would you mind going back outside and bring in that big bundle tied to the sled?"

When Johnny brought the bundle inside, Wild Bill explained, "This is the serum. We're supposed to unwrap it and let the bottles warm up so the serum doesn't freeze." Within a couple of minutes Johnny had the bottles of serum dangling from the ceiling over the wood stove. Wild Bill drank another cup of hot coffee and let the warmth seep through his body.

By seven o'clock Wild Bill was feeling much better and went outside to check on his dogs. What he saw shocked him. Three of the dogs were still so exhausted they couldn't stand up. It was 22 miles to the next relay site at Tolovana. Wild Bill knew those dogs would never make it. He and his dogs had been through a lot and he loved them dearly. But Wild Bill was a man who took his responsibilities seriously. His mission was to sled from Nenana to Tolovana and that was what he intended to do. He knew he couldn't wait for the three dogs to recover, so Wild Bill left them with Johnny. He would pick them up on his way home. With the serum carefully bundled up and tied to the sled, Wild Bill lifted the snowhook and took off. This time there were only six dogs in his team.

## CHAPTER 24

# Togo and Leonhard Head Out

At six o'clock that same morning, Mark Summers received word that the serum had left Nenana and was on its way toward Nome. He immediately called Leonhard Seppala and told him, "Leonhard, it's time to go."

Sigrid Seppala Hanks Collection, Carrie M. McLain Memorial Museum

Togo in single lead of a thirteen-dog team

As usual the Seppalas were prepared. Leonhard already had salmon and tallow for the dogs lashed to the sled. Constance had already cooked and packaged Leonhard's food. All that remained was to harness 20 dogs and head out. Leonhard spoke loudly over the din of barking dogs, "Constance, tell Mr. Summers I'm leaving 13 dogs here. That's enough for any freight hauling they might need to do. While I'm gone, use Fox as lead dog."

"Okay, I'll let him know," replied Constance.

Be prepared for everything, all the time — that was how Leonhard did things. He checked to make certain he had all his camping gear. Then he checked one last time to make sure that every single thing was tied down securely. He knew, even with Togo in lead, taking off with a team of 20 excited sled dogs and a light load meant that he would have little control at the start. He would only be able to stand on the back of the sled and hang on until the dogs settled down. Leonhard walked quickly over to Togo, who was doing his share of barking, and led him to the lead position. Togo did his best to stop bouncing around while his harness was put on. Next came Fritz, the dog who often ran beside Togo in lead. Togo knew his job was to stay up front and keep the gangline straight so the team dogs couldn't tangle themselves up. It was a tough job holding so many dogs straight but, with the help of Fritz, Togo made it happen. On such a long, dangerous, and important journey, Leonhard knew he might need extra leaders so he took lead dogs Billiken, Pete, and Young Scotty.

When all 20 dogs were hooked up, Leonhard stepped onto the runners. The dogs lunged forward, jerking the sled and threatening to break the snowhook loose. It was time to go. Constance stepped forward and gave him a quick hug. Sigrid stood on the porch and waved good bye. Leonhard reached down and lifted the snowhook. Instantly, the team shot forward. Only one thought went through Leonhard's brain - *whatever you do, don't fall off.*

About 20 minutes later, Togo and Fritz led the team into Nome and down the main street with heads held high. Word had spread that Leonhard Seppala would be passing through. People stood along the street waving and shouting words of encouragement. They knew he was heading out on a long and hazardous journey and that much was resting on his success. It was a great send-off and it meant a lot to Leonhard.

Compared to the Alaskan interior, conditions were nearly perfect. The temperature was 30 degrees below zero, there was little wind, and the trail was in excellent shape. The dogs continued running all out for a while longer and then settled into a ground-eating lope. They had hundreds of miles to go and Leonhard didn't want them to become too tired on the first day. So, although the dogs could have traveled much farther, Leonhard stopped after only 33 miles and spent the night at the roadhouse in Solomon.

CHAPTER 25

# The Race along the Yukon River

Back on the Yukon River.

About the time Leonhard and his team were hitting the trail, Wild Bill was leaving Minto. With only six dogs in his team, he couldn't travel very fast. To help the dogs, he often stood on one runner and used his other foot to help push the sled along. Sometimes he jumped off and ran along side. It helped speed the tired dogs and helped keep Wild Bill warm. Finally, after three and a half long, hard hours, the exhausted musher and dogs arrived in Tolovana.

Edgar Kallands was the next musher up. When Wild Bill and his team arrived, Edgar went outside to greet him along with the roadhouse owner and his family. One look at his dogs and the musher's frostbitten face told them all they needed to know. It had been a brutal journey. Wild Bill was so cold and stiff that he could hardly get off his sled. They quickly helped Wild Bill inside and gave him a cup of hot coffee and warm food. The serum was brought in and placed beside the stove to warm up. His dogs were quickly fed and bedded down.

It was a slow beginning, but from now on each relay team was assigned to carry the serum fewer miles. That allowed them to travel faster and the serum now started moving like an unstoppable freight train. Edgar Kallands had grown up in the brutally cold Alaskan interior. At twenty-one, he was already an experienced musher and mail driver. Undaunted by what had happened to Wild Bill, he stepped onto the back of his sled and took off down the Tanana River. Edgar Kallands was tough as nails and it didn't matter that the temperature was -56°F. His dogs sped along the trail through forest, across frozen swamps, and arrived later that day in Manley Hot Springs at about 4:00 p.m. It had taken Edgar and his dogs about five hours to travel 31 miles.

After the serum was warmed up in the roadhouse at Manley Hot Springs, Dan Green departed for Fish Lake in the late afternoon of January 28. Although it is only about 20 miles, the route was full of twists and turns curving around Manley Hot Springs Dome and along meandering creek beds that stretched the route to 28 miles. There were many trails that crisscrossed the area, but like every relay musher, Dan Green knew his part of the trail and never got off course.

Out of Fish Lake, Johnny Folger had the evening shift while driving in the dark along a forested trail. On most of the frozen lakes, the wind had blown the trail clear of snow. Sometimes the trail was nothing more than a scratch on the ice here and there. Like most dogs on the mail routes, Johnny's dogs knew the trail better than their driver. When Johnny couldn't see even a single scratch on the ice, he trusted his dogs. They never failed him over the entire 26 miles. He and his dogs made it to the village of Tanana where the Tanana River joins the mighty Yukon River.

The cold did not ease as Sam Joseph took possession of the serum in Tanana. Parts of the trail were through forests but sometimes the trail took him down onto the ice of the Yukon River. Travel on river ice is always dangerous. There are places where the ice is so thin a dog team can break through and fall into the water below. If that happens they will be swept away to their death by the powerful current. Usually the dogs can feel ice bending under their feet and will swerve to avoid thin ice. Courage is sledding through the night alone over river ice that might swallow you up in an instant. After 34 cold miles, Sam Joseph and his team arrived in the village of Kallands in the middle of the night. As it had been at every point in the relay, the serum was taken in and warmed before being handed off to the next musher.

Titus Nicholai was another man who knew his part of the route better than anyone else. It was not easy being alone in the cold and dark but Titus's courage never failed him. During the night of January 29, he sledded along the Yukon River but then cut across a huge slough, thereby saving many miles. Titus arrived at Nine Mile Cabin around daylight having traveled 24 miles. Because the serum was being transported over a series of relatively short distances, it was moving with amazing speed.

Next, Dave Corning took possession of the serum and headed off along the Yukon River. He cut across Hardluck Slough and traveled 30 miles to Kokrines, arriving around midday. From there Harry Pitka drove 30 miles around Hot Springs Slough, along the Yukon, and past Bootlegger Slough, arriving in the village of Ruby. Bill McCarty continued to speed the serum toward Nome, sledding along the river, past Mueller Mountain, reaching Whiskey Creek after 28 cold miles.

The next musher up was Edgar Nollner who raced 24 miles along the Yukon River. As he came round the bend, heading into his home village of Galena, he had an idea. When his brother, George, came out to greet him, Edgar said, "I think you should use my team. The dogs are still moving fast and you won't have to bother harnessing your dogs." George agreed. After warming the serum,

George sprinted through the bitterly cold night 18 miles to Bishop's Mountain.

Charlie Evans set out from Bishop's Mountain in the early morning light and moved quickly down the Yukon River. His dogs suffered from the intense cold. When he arrived in Nulato, his two leaders were riding in the sled. They had given their all and did not survive. It was a hard blow for Charlie but the serum was now 30 miles closer to Nome. After consoling Charlie and heating the serum for about half an hour, Tommy Patson took the serum on the last leg along the Yukon River. He covered 36 miles, arriving at Kaltag around midday on Friday, January 30.

In approximately two and one half days, the serum had been transported 391 miles from Nenana to Kaltag. No one team, no matter how fast, no one musher, no matter how experienced or knowledgeable, could possibly have accomplished that alone. This incredible feat was achieved through the cooperation, determination, and courage of 13 men and their tough, hard-working sled dogs.

# CHAPTER 26

# The Serum Reaches the Coast

Where was Leonhard Seppala? Back when Titus Nicholai was arriving at Nine Mile Cabin early on the morning of January 29, Leonhard Seppala was leaving Solomon on his second day of travel. The telephone lines only went as far as Solomon and then cut directly across Norton Sound to St. Michael. From there the lines went north only as far as Unalakleet and then over the Kaltag Portage to Kaltag on the Yukon River.

Unfortunately, Leonhard had already left Solomon before word could reach him about the change in plans. He had no way of knowing about the relay that was speeding the serum toward him. As far as he knew, he still had to sled all the way to Nulato. The powers that be back in Nome had lost control of the relay. All they could do now was hope that by some miracle, the Nome-bound musher and Leonhard would find one another out there on the trail.

Out of Solomon Leonhard took the trail along the north shore of Norton Sound. After a few miles he saw that the sea ice had shattered and been forced up onto the beach. Not wanting the dogs to get injured, Leonhard commanded Togo to take them out onto Norton Sound where the ice was a little more stable. The temperature continued to fall as the wind steadily rose. Togo picked his way along and led the team around pile after pile of jumbled ice. At the end of a difficult day, they headed back to land. Still believing they had hundreds of miles ahead of them, Leonhard stopped after only 45 miles and spent the night in the village of Chinik.

On the morning of January 30, Togo lead the team out of Chinik. They stayed on land for several miles before heading back out onto the sea ice of Norton Sound. Leonhard and Togo were very familiar with this area. Leonhard knew traveling on the sea ice out around Bald Head to reach Isaac's Point was always dangerous. If a strong wind started blowing away from shore, the ice could break off and carry Leonhard and the dogs out to sea. But luck was with them, the wind was blowing toward land, keeping the ice against the shore. After 53 miles, Togo led the team to shore at Isaac's Point. They had now traveled 130 miles from Nome.

While Leonhard and his team had been heading toward Isaac's Point, a fellow by the curious name of Jackscrew was starting over the Kaltag Portage. This

90-mile portage leads up and over a chain of mountains from Kaltag to Unalakleet. The trail has been used by people going back and forth from the Interior to the coast for centuries. It was a well-used and well-marked trail. Jackscrew and his dogs labored up a steep incline for about 15 miles. They then traveled another 35 miles on a fairly flat trail during daylight. Jackscrew and his dogs arrived at a shelter cabin known as Old Woman Cabin, where he brought the serum inside to be warmed up.

Victor Anagick already had the cabin toasty warm. He and Jackscrew visited for about half an hour while they warmed the serum. Then Victor left Old Woman Cabin and mushed 40 miles, making the difficult, steep downhill run to the coastal village of Unalakleet. It was January 31. Up until now the mushers and their dogs had faced dangerous river ice, navigated obscure trails through the dark of night, climbed up and over a mountain range, and did their part through mind numbing cold. Never once did anyone think about giving up.

The serum had reached the coast. Now there was a new challenge, the biggest challenge of all. The serum had to be transported across Norton Sound. Cold was the enemy in the Interior, but here on the coast, the enemy was wind. Often raging at 70 miles per hour (hurricane speed), the wind could shove a team completely out of control sideways, forward, and even backwards. It could blast a musher right off his sled. It could flip his sled over and over. If that happened, all the musher could do was hang on to the handlebar with all his might. If a musher became separated from the team in such wind, it almost certainly meant death by freezing. Then there was the ice itself. The wind could move it but so could powerful currents under the ice. Sometimes those currents were strong enough to break a huge piece of ice in half. A channel of water called a lead would open up between the two pieces. Leads were sometimes only three or four feet wide and easily crossed. But they could be up to half a mile wide, leaving the musher and team trapped on the ice floe. What the currents could tear asunder, they could thrust together. When two enormous pieces of ice collided, long ridges of ice called pressure ridges formed. They were often more than ten feet high and difficult to climb over. There were other places where the ice broke and then piled up in vast stretches of jumbled ice only a few feet high. This created a chaos of ice that was nearly impossible to sled through.

On Norton Sound the wind never stops blowing and the ice never stops moving. If the wind wasn't shoving the ice around, it often blew so much snow into the air that it became impossible for the musher to see his dogs. Sometimes the wind blew the snow completely away exposing patches of glare ice. This ice was so slick the dogs could hardly stand up let alone pull a sled. When a musher sets out over Norton Sound, he could only rely on experience, instincts, and his dogs.

## CHAPTER 27

# Crossing Norton Sound

It was very early in the morning on January 31 when Myles Gonangnan got the serum from Victor Anagick and prepared to leave Unalakleet. He had a very difficult decision to make. Which route should he take to cross Norton Sound?

Myles Gonangnan was twenty-eight years old and had lived in Unalakleet his entire life. He knew he had only two choices. He could head straight across Norton Sound from Unalakleet and hope to find Leonhard somewhere out on the ice, or he could sled up the coast and set out from the village of Shaktoolik.

The problem was that no one knew where Leonhard was right then. But because no one had run into him yet, Gonangnan knew that Leonhard could not have crossed Norton Sound. He also knew the area well enough to know that Leonhard would almost certainly set out from Isaac's Point.

Gonangnan stood on the shore looking out over Norton Sound, studying the ice and wind. This time of year powerful winds blew almost constantly. If it came from the west, it would shove the ice toward land. But if, as usual, it came from the east or northeast, it would push the ice out to sea. The weather made the decision for Gonangnan. The wind was out of the northeast and steadily increasing. He knew from experience that a storm was coming very soon. Though the sun would not rise for another six hours, under the faint light of a first-quarter moon, Gonangnan could see the ice was already heaving and starting to break up. He made the only reasonable choice. He would sled up the coast 40 miles to Shaktoolik and try his best to get there before the storm struck. With the decision made, Gonangnan quickly harnessed his dogs, strapped the serum to the sled, and headed north along the coast.

Several inches of new snow made for a tough pull. Gonangnan's dogs were big, heavy freight dogs and were used for pulling big loads in all kinds of weather. They were plodders and usually traveled only four or five miles per hour. As they slogged through the snowdrifts, punching through at nearly every step, they didn't slow down. In places where the wind had blown the trail clear, they didn't speed up. They just kept plodding along, up and down across the rolling hills.

After about 25 miles they came to the settlement of Egavik where Gonangnan rested the dogs and warmed the serum. By the time he got back onto the trail the storm was moving in. The wind was blowing so much snow across the land that everything, trees, horizon, even the trail, appeared as though they were behind a thin, white curtain. The wind kept increasing until they were in a white-out. The earth, the sky, even the trail itself now blended together. There was no sense of direction or speed. Myles Gonangnan and his dogs had been in this kind of situation many times. They were tough and used to the horrific conditions along the coast. The dogs knew the trail and he never doubted they would get him through. After nine hours of sledding through brutal weather, the serum was now in Shaktoolik.

That same morning, January 31, a few hours after Myles Gonangnan had set out from Unalakleet, Leonhard Seppala stood beside Togo looking out over Norton Sound. He still thought they had 225 miles to travel before they would reach Nulato. Then he would turn the team around and sled 355 miles back to Nome. As he stood looking out over the sea ice, Leonhard had a critical decision to make. There were two choices. They could sled along the shore of Norton Sound where travel would be safer or they could cross the sound on the sea ice. Either way had risks. If they kept to the coast it would mean an additional day's travel and take longer to get the serum to Nome. More people might die. Leonhard knew if they headed across the sea ice, it would be half the miles of the coastal route. Right then the wind was out of the northwest. But if the wind shifted to the east or northeast, the ice could break up. They could end up on an island of ice and float around for days before making it back to land. In fact, they might be swept out to sea and never make it back. They could die out there.

It played heavily on Leonhard's mind that his daughter, Sigrid, would be at risk until she was vaccinated. Leonhard was a thinking man and he tried not to let his concern for Sigrid affect his decision. He must rely on logic. The wind was growing stronger but it continued out of the northwest. That meant it would be at their backs if they crossed Norton Sound. He looked down at Togo and said, "It's worth the risk, Togo. We're going to cross on the ice."

Togo and Young Scotty were in lead. They knew their job and the moment Leonhard gave the command, the two dogs led the team straight out onto the ice. As they moved along, the wind kept increasing and Leonhard knew a storm was coming. Soon hard grains of snow and tiny pieces of thin, crusty ice were blowing across the sound. Leonhard thought to himself, *If we'd gone around on the coast we would never have made it to Shaktoolik before this storm hits. This was the right choice.*

The team moved in a southeasterly direction. With the wind at his back and pulling a light sled, Togo felt so exhilarated that he started running. He enjoyed the excitement of tearing around jumbled ice and racing across stretches of flat ice. The other dogs felt the excitement and the joy of running with the wind. They practically flew across the ice.

When they arrived at the fish camp of Ungalik on the east side of Norton Sound, Leonhard let out a long sigh of relief. He stopped the team in the shelter of a cabin and gave them all a little snack. He rubbed the dog's ears and necks and told them, "You did a great job. We made another 20 miles. Shaktoolik is only 23 miles away and that is over land." As the dogs rested, Leonhard looked at the sky and muttered to himself, "I just hope we get there before the storm shows up."

## CHAPTER 28

# "The Serum! The Serum!"

As they neared Shaktoolik, the wind began to shift as the storm started closing in. All of Leonhard's dogs had been over this trail before and they knew a village was close. That meant a big meal and a good night's rest. With that knowledge in their sled dog brains, Leonhard didn't have to ask them to speed up, they just did it on their own.

Crazy as it may seem, Henry Ivanoff had been instructed to head out from Shaktoolik with the serum into the worsening storm in hopes of finding Leonhard, even though no one knew where Leonhard and his team were or what route they had taken to cross Norton Sound. Henry had only made it a short distance out of Shaktoolik when his dogs spotted a herd of reindeer. They took off like a shot. By the time Henry managed to get them stopped, they were in such a frenzy, the entire team got into a huge fight. Wading into a team to break up a fight is likely to get the musher bitten. Nevertheless, that's exactly what Henry was doing when he spotted a team coming his way. Leonhard's Siberian Huskies were distinctive in appearance and Henry knew immediately that it had to be Leonhard Seppala on that sled!

Leonhard had already gone past Henry when he thought he heard the word "serum". The wind was blowing hard and had swept Henry's voice away. Leonhard turned his head and looked back. He saw a man frantically waving at him and now he caught what the man was shouting - "Serum! Serum! I have the serum!"

In that moment all Leonhard's dogs were thinking about was that big meal and nice long rest that lay just ahead. "Whoa!" called Leonhard. "Whoa!" Togo glanced back but could not understand why Leonhard would possibly want to stop. As luck would have it, in that moment they came to a large patch of hard, wind-packed snow. Leonhard jammed the sled brake into the snow and managed to get the team stopped.

"Togo, come gee," he commanded. Togo looked back and saw the team in a big fight. He hesitated. Togo didn't like dog fights. "Togo! Come gee!" Togo had no idea what Leonhard was thinking but he swung the team around to the right and headed them toward the brawling team.

When they got close to Henry's team, the dogs had finally stopped fighting. But Togo decided to play it safe and stopped several feet from where Henry stood. Henry lifted the package out of his sled and brought it over to Leonhard. "The epidemic has worsened," he said. "At least five people have died and a lot more are sick. They got a bunch of mushers to form a relay to speed the serum up and they got it as far as Shaktoolik. I was heading out to find you when my dogs got into a fight." Henry explained the warming instructions as Leonhard lashed the bundle to his sled.

"Okay, Henry. We won't go to Shaktoolik, we'll start back to Nome right now," said Leonhard.

Henry turned his team around, waved good bye, and returned to Shaktoolik. Leonhard knew that the relay had gotten the serum to Shaktoolik, but he still thought he was the only one who would carry it 170 miles back to Nome.

"Togo, Young Scotty, sorry but we won't be resting anytime soon. We have to head back to Nome right now."

Without hesitation, Togo and Young Scotty headed into the wind and blowing snow. By the time they traveled 23 miles back to Ungalik, the wind had shifted and was coming out of the northeast. In this region the most violent storms come from the northeast, especially during January and February. For drivers attempting to cross Norton Sound, those storms are the most feared of all. They race right down the sound, break the ice away from shore, and shove it out to sea. Once again Leonhard was faced with the same critical decision. Should they cross Norton Sound on the ice or go around on the coast?

CHAPTER 29

# Life and Death

Back in Nome there were three new cases of diphtheria. At least 30 more people might have it and an unknown number had likely been exposed to the deadly disease. Dr. Welch had used all the serum available in Nome. The members of the Board of Health were beside themselves with worry. The last they knew the serum had left Unalakleet. But where was Leonhard Seppala? Where was the serum?

Mark Summers came up with yet another idea that involved sled dogs. He believed Leonhard and his dogs must surely be heading back to Nome by now. He set up an additional relay that would go from Chinik to Nome. He ordered Ed Rohn and his racing team to travel to Safety and wait. Gunnar Kaasen was instructed to drive a team past Safety to Bluff. Kaasen's team was made up of dogs Leonhard had left behind at his kennel. Upon arriving at Bluff, Kaasen was to enlist the help of Charlie Olson who would drive his team to Chinik. There Charlie would wait for Leonhard to arrive.

Leonhard Seppala stood at Ungalik on the shore of Norton Sound. If they crossed from here they would be traveling northwest. The storm had arrived. Every minute the wind was growing stronger. If they started across the sound from Ungalik, the wind would strike them from the side with horrific force. The ice still looked fairly stable but Leonhard could see it was beginning to move. Soon the ice would break up and there would be huge areas of open water.

It was late afternoon and the light was fading fast. Leonhard knew he wouldn't be able to see in the dark out on the ice. He knew he wouldn't smell open water soon enough to avoid driving into it. But dogs see better in the dark than people and they have a better sense of smell. Togo would be able to see out there and he would smell open water. The trail had already disappeared under drifting snow. But Togo had been this way many times before. Togo was a brilliant, experienced lead dog and he knew exactly where the trail was. Leonhard knew if they were going to make it across alive, he had to trust Togo.

He began talking out loud, "We have to try, Togo. We're going straight across."

Togo cocked his head to one side as if to say, *Well alright then. Let's get going!*

Leonhard took the tug line off Togo's harness and set him free. He walked back to the sled, climbed onto the runners, and said, "Togo, take us home."

Togo lowered his nose to the snow, sniffed, and took off across the ice. The wind was growing stronger every second. At times the wind blew so hard, Togo had to lower himself onto his belly just to keep from being blown away. Leonhard could feel the ice shifting and heaving under the sled. Even above the roar of the wind he could hear the ugly sound of ice grinding and breaking. Suddenly they passed a dark shadow on their left — open water! The ice of Norton Sound was breaking up right underneath them!

Somehow in the darkness, Togo managed to find a way to keep going. Running loose, Togo led the team around every stretch of open water and over every pile of jumbled ice. Across the entire 20 miles, running at a steady nine miles per hour in gale force winds of over 40 mph, at 30 degrees below zero, Togo never made a single mistake. Just after 8 pm, Togo led the team right up to the front door of Isaac's Roadhouse. They had made it. They were safe.

Leonhard would later say he thought that somehow Togo understood the urgency of the situation. That is very possible because sled dogs can certainly tell when their driver is stressed. At times like that, they will do their job without causing any problems. Leonhard would have felt tremendous stress upon learning that the epidemic was worsening and that Sigrid and Constance were still in grave danger. Togo would have picked up on that.

The Eskimo family at Isaac's Point quickly fed Leonhard and the dogs. They hauled the entire sled inside to warm up the serum and put Leonhard to bed. Exhausted though he was, Leonhard asked to be awakened at 2:00 a.m. As requested they woke him up and helped him harness the team.

"How will you go?" asked the Eskimo man.

Leonhard said, "We came around Bald Head on the ice, so we'll go back the same way."

"Maybe that's not a good idea. The storm is going to break the ice loose anytime now. It's too dangerous to go that way. Maybe you should go the inland route."

Leonhard respected the Eskimo and his knowledge of the area and appreciated his concern.

"That's good advice. We'll go that way."

The storm was still raging as Leonhard climbed onto the runners. Togo expected they would keep going back to Nome the way they had come. He knew the route and was ready to head out onto the ice. When Leonhard commanded him to go right and head back into the hills, Togo was surprised but he didn't argue.

It was wise to follow the advice given him by the

Eskimo. A few hours later, while Togo was leading them through the hills behind Bald Head, the ice broke off and was blown out to sea.

As Togo led the team back down to the coast, the blizzard continued to worsen. The blowing snow made it almost impossible to see. There was no place to take shelter from the brutal wind. Leonhard could see the dogs were stiffening up and beginning to freeze. He stopped the team. Leonhard dropped to his knees and used his body to shelter the wheel dogs from the wind. He rubbed their legs and bellies to help keep the circulation going. One by one, he crawled past each dog helping them as best he could. But his best was not enough. They had to keep going or they would die. Leonhard climbed onto the sled and called "All right, Togo, let's go!"

Finally, they left the coast and cut inland toward Chinik. After 13 hours and 48 miles of misery, Togo lead the team to Dexter's Roadhouse. Leonhard was surprised to see Charlie Olson there. Charlie explained that Mark Summers had sent teams out to Safety, Bluff, and Chinik to help get the serum to Nome as quickly as possible. It was no slight to Leonhard and his dogs. They had traveled a total of 264 miles in four and a half days. Of that, 91 miles were from Shaktoolik to Chinik, over the longest, most hazardous part of the trail in horrific, life-threatening weather. Leonhard knew his dogs were exhausted and needed rest. He was only too happy to hand the serum over to Charlie.

# CHAPTER 30

# The Race To Nome

The serum was taken inside and warmed up. When Charlie was ready to leave he looked outside. It was almost dark and the blizzard was still raging. Like every one of the 20 men who took part in this race for life, Charlie Olson did not hesitate. He climbed onto his sled and headed for Bluff, 25 miles away. The blizzard grew even more powerful. It was so cold, that Charlie had to stop and put little blankets on his dogs to keep them from freezing. By the time he finished caring for his dogs, Charlie's hands and face were badly frostbitten. There was nothing more he could do for his dogs, so they kept going.

Gunnar Kaasen was waiting at Bluff for Charlie and his dogs. Kaasen planned to head out as soon as the serum was warmed. But when he saw what terrible condition Charlie and his dogs were in, he decided to stay and help care for them. After two hours Charlie was doing better. When Kaasen set out around 9:30 p.m. that night, the wind was blowing but the storm was starting to let up.

Over in Nome, Mark Summers was so concerned about the storm and the safety of the mushers, he sent messages by telephone to Safety and Solomon calling a halt to the relay until the storm was over. Ed Rohn expected that if Kaasen didn't stop at Solomon, he would stop at Safety. Ed went to bed, thinking he would take the serum into Nome the next day.

Kaasen did not stop in Solomon. When he arrived at Safety, he saw no light in the cabin, so he assumed Ed was asleep. By now the storm was pretty well over. The moon was half full, providing fairly good light. Kaasen thought it would take too much time to wake Ed and get his dogs harnessed. So, he decided to keep going the last 53 miles to Nome.

Because the relay was supposed to have been stopped, no one was expecting the serum to arrive until later that day. Gunnar Kaasen arrived in Nome at 5:30 a.m., February 2, 1925. Nome was still under quarantine and the streets were deserted. There were no witnesses.

No one was more surprised to see Kaasen than Dr. Welch when he was awakened on that frosty morning. Kaasen handed the bundle to Dr. Welch and together they went inside. When they opened the bundle, they found the serum was frozen solid. Dr. Welch had anticipated this. He had already been in touch with the serum manufacturer who assured him that the serum would still be usable.

Getting the serum delivered was only the first step in saving the people of Nome. Once the serum was thawed, nurses Emily Morgan and Bertha Saville put on their heavy, winter clothes and trudged out through the snow to vaccinate the people who were most at risk. Throughout the epidemic, these two brave women repeatedly exposed themselves to diphtheria by continuing to visit the sick. As nurses, they saw this as their duty and never complained. Their bravery and loyalty to their patients earned them the trust and respect of everyone on the Sandspit and in Nome. Wherever they went they were welcomed as they made their lifesaving rounds.

Of course the 300,000 units that arrived via relay were not nearly enough to vaccinate everyone. The additional 1.1 million units of serum reached the ice-free port of Seward and the entire serum relay was done all over again. Most of the heroes who took part in that second run never received any recognition but they did their jobs just like the men of the first relay. Within a month the diphtheria epidemic had been halted. Nome was saved.

In his unpublished autobiography, Leonhard Seppala wrote, "Afterwards I thought of the ice and the darkness and the terrible wind and the irony that men could build planes and ships, but when Nome needed life in little packages of serum, it took the dogs to bring it through."

## CHAPTER 31

# Togo Is Gone!

After Leonhard turned the serum over to Charlie Olson, he and his tired dogs spent the night resting in Chinik. The next morning, Leonhard put a weary Togo in lead, harnessed up the rest of the dogs, and set out for Nome. Somewhere along the trail they came within sight of a herd of reindeer. Togo swung around, bit his tug line in two, and took off after them.

"Togo, come back here!"

Togo stopped and looked back at Leonhard. He remembered that day almost nine years ago when, as an eight month old puppy, he had gotten loose and run off to find Leonhard. On that day he had seen a herd of reindeer and decided to chase them. It was a special day. An exciting day. It was the day he made Leonhard's team.

Now just a few miles from home, Leonhard stood beside his sled looking at Togo. He could see it in Togo's eyes. Some days Togo just had a mind of his own and today was one of those days. Leonhard called Togo to come back but he knew it was pointless. Today Togo was going to chase reindeer. Togo took off across the tundra and disappeared over the horizon.

Togo was gone.

Leonhard wanted badly to chase after Togo and get him back. He knew that a dog chasing reindeer could be legally shot by reindeer herders and he knew there were traps everywhere. But Leonhard was still very worried about Sigrid and Constance. So, with Young Scotty and Billiken in lead, he headed for home. When they arrived in Nome on February 2, it was a very cold day. Even so, about 200 people swarmed Leonhard and the dogs and thanked them for all they had done to help save the town.

Much to Leonhard's relief, Sigrid and Constance were fine. But Leonhard was beside himself with worry about Togo. He immediately hired several men to go out and try to find him.

Meanwhile back on the tundra, Togo was probably having himself quite an adventure. Of course, chasing reindeer over miles of open country would have lost its appeal after a while. Then he probably went back to the trail and spent a few days walking back and forth looking for Leonhard. When he couldn't find Leonhard, Togo apparently decided to take himself home. On February 10 a mail driver spotted Togo walking along the trail heading toward Nome. The man put Togo in his team in lead and made it to Nome in record time.

When Leonhard received a call that Togo was at the Post Office, he hooked up a small team and rushed down to get him. He found Togo sitting on a snowbank tied to the mail driver's sled. As Leonhard walked up to him, their eyes met. "We've been missing you, Togo." Togo swished his tail back and forth.

"Woof!"

Leonhard hooked Togo into the gangline and they headed home. The dogs at the kennel sat like little statues watching the team approaching. When they realized it was Togo in lead, every dog started barking and running in circles. Constance and Sigrid ran out to join in the excitement. Sigrid gave Togo a hug. Constance gave Leonhard a hug. Togo was safe! Togo was home! It was a joyful day at the Leonhard Seppala kennel.

# EPILOGUE

During the serum run Togo gave Leonhard everything he had. Some say he gave too much. It's true that he never again took part in any of Leonhard's long trips, but from time to time he did compete in a few short races.

In 1926, Leonhard began going back East almost every year, talking to thousands of people across the country about the need to get vaccinated against diphtheria. He always took Togo and many of his other dogs with him. In Maine he became good friends with musher Peg Ricker. Togo and Peg also took a liking to one another. Because Togo was getting on in years, Leonhard thought Togo would be better off if he stayed in the gentler climate of Maine instead of returning to Alaska. So, on February 6, 1927, Leonhard left Togo with Peg. She gave Togo love, kindness, and excellent care for the rest of his life.

Sigrid Seppala Hanks Collection, Carrie M. McLain Memorial Museum

Leonhard says good bye to Togo as he leaves him to live in the milder climate of Maine with friend Peg Ricker.

# *Glossary*

ANTI-TOXIN: An antibody that reduces or eliminates the effects of a toxin

BRUSH BOW: A piece of wood or plastic that wraps around the front of a dog sled

CACHE: A place where provisions are placed for later use

COME GEE: The command that tells the dog to turn around to the right and go back the direction it came from

COME HAW: The command that tells a dog to turn around to the left and go back the direction it came from

COMMANDS: The words used by mushers to tell their lead dogs what to do

DIPHTHERIA: A bacteria disease of the mucous membranes in the nose and throat

DOG DRIVER: A person who sits on a dog sled and commands a dog team, also called a musher

GANGLINE: A system of ropes running from the front of a dogsled. The dogs are clipped into the gangline by short lines called tug lines.

GEE: The command that tells a dog to go right

GLARE ICE: Smooth, glassy ice that is usually very slick and difficult to stand up on

HAW: The command that tells a dog to turn left

HYPOTHERMIA: A condition in which the body becomes too cold to maintain its normal temperature and shuts down the flow of blood to hands and feet, then arms and legs, in an attempt to keep vital organs warm

LEAD: An opening of water in sea, river, or lake ice

MOUNT McKINLEY: The tallest mountain in North America. Its formal name has been changed to Denali.

MUSH: To be pulled over snow and ice on a sled pulled by dogs

MUSHER: A person who rides on a dog sled and commands the dog team, also called a dog driver

PRESSURE RIDGE: A ridge of ice, commonly ranging in height from a few inches up to twenty feet or more, formed by the pressure of expending or shifting ice

PTARMIGAN: A species of northern grouse with feathered legs

RELAY: A series of persons or animals used to relieve one another on a journey

SALMON: A kind of edible fish with pink flesh

SEA ICE: Ice that forms when ocean water freezes

SERUM RUN: A term coined to describe the series of 20 dog teams that carried anti-toxin 474 miles from Nenana to Nome during the diphtheria epidemic of 1925

SIBERIAN HUSKY: A medium-size breed of dog with a thick, soft coat, erect ears, and a bushy tail originating from Siberia. They are known for being friendly, hard-working, and are often used to pull a dog sled.

SLED BAG: A heavy cloth bag that is placed in the sled basket and cinched tightly to contain gear and keep snow out

SLED BASKET: The main body of the sled where passengers or cargo are carried

SLED BRAKE: A two or three-pronged metal claw attached to the floor of the sled used to stop or slow the sled when pressed down by one foot. A spring holds the brake up when not in use.

SNOWHOOK: A large, heavy, two-pronged, iron hook, attached to the sled with a rope, that is used to anchor the sled by jamming the prongs into the snow

TALLOW: A kind of hard fat

TOW LINE: The line that runs down the middle of a gangline and is attached to the sled

TUG LINE: A rope that is attached at one end to the end of a dog's harness and the other end to the gangline

TUNDRA: Treeless plains in the arctic with low-growing vegetation on top of cold, often frozen ground

WHITEOUT: A condition in which light is reflected almost equally from the sky above and the snow below so that almost no shadows are cast, causing the snow and sky to blend into total whiteness

# Source Material*

*Alaska Railroad Record.* Alaska Railroad, Vol IV, #29 p232

Blake, Robert. *Togo.* Philomel Books, 2002

*Caterpillar Times.* February, 1921 p 12

*Epidemiology and Prevention of Vaccine Preventable Diseases* 13th edition. Center for Disease Control and Prevention

*Diphtheria.* Harrison's Principals of Internal Medicine. 1978

Dunham, Mike. *Emily's mission: Dispensing the famous Nome serum.* Anchorage Daily News. March 15, 2011

Harrington, John. *Across Bering Strait On The Ice.* Indians At Work, The U.S. Department of the Interior 1938

Hawley, Charles. *Jafet Lindeberg.* Alaska Mining Hall of Fame, 1998

Head, Bruce. *A History of Dog Sledding in New England.* History Press Library, 2011

Jacobs, Mina. *Beeson, John, M.D.* Cook Inlet Historical Society, 2012.

Madsen , Charles, and John Douglas. *Arctic Trader.* Dodd, Mead 1957

Miller, Debbie S. *The Great Serum Race.* Bloomsbury USA Children's, 2006

*Nome Nugget* - multiple articles

Orth, Donald. *Dictionary of Alaska Place Names.* U.S. Geologic Survey Publication, 1971

Ricker, Elizabeth. *Fireside.* Lewiston Journal Printshop, 1928

Ricker, Elizabeth. *Seppala: Alaskan Dog Driver.* Kessinger Publishing, 1930

*Rivers & Harbors Hearings* U.S. Congress House Committee, 1930

Rozell, Ned. *Innoko is a Long River Short on People.* UAF News and Information, 2019

Salisbury, Gay, and Laney Salisbury. *The Cruelest Miles.* W. W. Norton & Company, 2005

Seppala, Constance. *The Golden Jubilee of Dog Racing*

Seppala, Constance. *Togo the Sled Dog* (unpublished)

Seppala, Leonhard. *The Musher.* International Siberian Husky Club March/April, 1997

Seppala, Leonhard and Raymond Thompson. *I met my first Dog Team 60 years ago*. Raymond Thompson

Seppala, Leonhard. *Unpublished Autobiography*

Seppala, Leonhard, and Raymond Thompson. *When Nome Needed Serum.*

Sherwonit, Bill, and Peter Bowers. *Dog of the North*. Alaska Geographic Society 1987.

Thomas, Bob and Pam Thomas. *Leonhard Seppala: The Siberian Dog and The Golden Age of Sleddog Racing 1908-1941* Pictorial Histories Publishing Company, 2015

Thompson, Raymond. *Seppala's Saga of the Sled Dog*. Raymond Thompson, 1970

U.S. Congressional Serial Set, Volume 4762, 1900-14

Ungermann, Kenneth. *The Race to Nome*. Harper & Row, 1963

Welch, Dr. Curtis. *The diphtheria Epidemic at Nome* Journal of the American Medical Association, 1925

Widrig, Charlotte. *The Golden Days of Dogsled Racing.* Seattle Times *March 28, 1954*

- Not all dates were found.